For more than forty years,
Yearling has been the leading name
in classic and award-winning literature
for young readers.

Yearling books feature children's
favorite authors and characters,
providing dynamic stories of adventure,
humor, history, mystery, and fantasy.

Trust Yearling paperbacks to entertain,
inspire, and promote the love of reading
in all children.

Boston Jane

AN ADVENTURE

JENNIFER L. HOLM

A YEARLING BOOK

Copyright © 2001 by Jennifer L. Holm

All rights reserved. Published in the United States by Yearling, an imprint of Random House Children's Books, a division of Random House, Inc., New York. Originally published in hardcover in the United States by HarperCollins Children's Books, a division of HarperCollins Publishers, New York, in 2001.

Yearling and the jumping horse design are registered trademarks of Random House, Inc.

Visit us on the Web! www.randomhouse.com/kids

Educators and librarians, for a variety of teaching tools, visit us at
www.randomhouse.com/teachers

Library of Congress Cataloging-in-Publication Data
Holm, Jennifer L.
Boston Jane: an adventure / by Jennifer L. Holm. — 1st trade pbk. ed.
p. cm.
Sequel: Boston Jane: wilderness days.
Summary: Schooled in the lessons of etiquette for young ladies of 1854,
Miss Jane Peck of Philadelphia finds little use for manners during her long
sea voyage to the Pacific Northwest and while living among the American
traders and Chinook Indians of Washington Territory.
ISBN 978-0-375-86204-5 (trade pbk.) — ISBN 978-0-375-96204-2 (lib. bdg.) —
ISBN 978-0-375-89399-5 (e-book)
[1. Self-perception—Fiction. 2. Etiquette—Fiction.
3. Chinook Indians—Fiction. 4. Indians of North America—Washington (State)—Fiction.
5. Frontier and pioneer life—Washington (State)—Fiction. 6. Washington
Territory—History—19th century—Fiction.] I. Title.
PZ7.H732226Bo 2010
[Fic]—dc21
2009004847

Printed in the United States of America

10 9 8 7 6 5 4 3 2 1

First Yearling Edition

ACKNOWLEDGMENTS

Writers are explorers, but like all explorers, we need guides to help us find our way in the wilderness.

I have been very fortunate to have fantastic guides for *Boston Jane*. First, and foremost, a big thank-you to my terrific editors, Elise Howard and Ginee Seo, for believing in Jane. I have the nicest agent in the world, Jill Grinberg, and I can't thank her enough for her good advice. And a million thanks to Shana Corey, Kate Klimo, Mallory Loehr, Heather Palisi, Diane João, and the whole gang at Random House for taking this adventure with Jane.

A lot of research went into this book and many kind and generous people read the manuscript. I'd especially like to thank Gary Johnson, chairman of the Chinook Tribe, for giving thoughtful and excellent notes. Bruce Weilepp and Diantha Weilepp of the Pacific County Historical Society were incredibly patient with my long-winded questions (as always). And John O'Donnell was invaluable regarding nineteenth-century Philadelphia.

Joan Mann at the Ilwaco Museum Research Library was wonderful with Willapa Bay queries. Scott Eberle and Carol Sandler at the Strong

Museum were fantastic resources on just about everything American! In addition to being an excellent resource on nineteenth-century medicine, Sara Cleary-Burns and Stanley Burns of the Burns Archive were wonderfully supportive friends. Judy Downey and Laura Pereira at the New Bedford Whaling Museum and James Delgado at the Vancouver Maritime Museum helped with my nautical research.

Most of all I'd like to thank Paul and Ginny Merz, the *Boston Jane* Willapa Bay Research Team, for their incredible support—I could never have done it without you! You guys are the best!

My family has been very supportive, especially my dad, who faithfully read each and every draft, and my youngest brother, Matt, a fine writer himself, who went the extra mile and helped me with all the little details that bedevil writers. And, of course, my mom, who helped me survive my very own Sally Biddle.

I want to thank some inspirational librarians and educators for their generous advice and friendship, especially Carolyn Brodie, Maria Salvadore, Diane Ellenburg, Elizabeth Poe, and Mary Ann Paulin. Also some great writers—Chris Curtis and Jerry Spinelli—for being so kind to the new girl! And of course, Ralph and Martha Slotten and Rudy and Diane Cusumano—good teachers every one, and even better friends.

And the biggest thank-you to Louise and Willard Espy for inspiring me to write this book in the first place!

Finally I must thank my husband, Jonathan, for his endless good advice, taking me to the Dixie Chicks concert for inspiration when I was stuck, and overall great husbandness in all things (especially the kissing part).

It's always good to do the research firsthand!

For Jonathan,
who loved Jane
from the first

If you are a well-bred lady, you must carry
your good manners everywhere with you.
It is not a thing that can be laid aside
and put on at pleasure.

—THE YOUNG LADY'S FRIEND (1836),
By a Lady

CHAPTER ONE
or,
Miss Hepplewhite's Opinion

Papa always said you make your own luck.

But after being seasick for five months, two weeks, and six days, I felt certain that luck had nothing to do with anything aboard the *Lady Luck*, a poorly named vessel if ever there was one. I had just spent the morning of my sixteenth birthday puking into a bucket, and I had little hope that the day would improve.

I had no doubt that I was the unluckiest young lady in the world.

It wasn't always this way.

Once I was the luckiest girl in the world.

When I was eleven years old, in 1849, the sea seemed to me a place of great wonder. I would lie on my four-poster bed in my room overlooking the street and pretend I was on one of the sleek ships that sailed along the waterfront, returning from exotic, faraway places like China and the Sandwich Islands and Liverpool.

When the light shone through the window a certain watery way, it was easy to imagine that I was bobbing gently on the waves of the ocean, the air around me warm and sweet and tinged with salt.

We lived on Walnut Street, in a brick house with green shutters, just steps from the State House. Heavy silk drapes hung in the windows, and there was new gas lighting in every room. When the lights were on, it glowed like fairyland. I believed it to be the loveliest house in all of Philadelphia, if only because we lived there.

And my father was the most wonderful father in Philadelphia—or perhaps the whole world.

Each morning Papa would holler, "Where is my favorite daughter?"

I would leap out of bed and rush to the top of the stairs, my feet bare, my hair a frightful mess.

"She is right here!" I would shout. "And she is your *only* daughter!"

"You're not my Janey," he would roar, his white beard shaking, his belly rolling with laughter. "My Janey's not a slugabed! My Janey's hair is never tangled!"

My mother had died giving birth to me, so it had only ever been Papa and me. Papa always said that one wild, redheaded daughter was enough for any sane man.

As for my sweet papa, how can I describe the wisest of men? Imagine all that is good and dear and generous, and that was my papa.

Papa was a surgeon, the finest in all of Philadelphia. He took me on rounds with him to visit his patients. I was always proud to hold the needle and thread while he stitched up a man who had been beaten in a bar brawl. Or I would sit on a man's belly while Papa set a broken leg. Papa said a man behaved better and didn't scream so much when a little girl was sitting on his belly.

I was the luckiest girl.

How could I not be with Mrs. Parker's cherry pie?

Mrs. Parker was our housekeeper, and she made the best cherry pie in the entire world. I ate it at every opportunity. Papa always said that I was going to turn into a cherry pie myself one day if I wasn't careful.

This was Mrs. Parker's cherry pie: all tangy cherries rolled up in a golden, buttery crust. It was as sweet as clean sheets on washing day, as warm as the chair by the kitchen stove on a cold afternoon. Just imagine it sitting on the plate waiting for you, all piping hot from the oven.

"There is nothing better in the world than a slice of Mrs. Parker's cherry pie after a long day of stitching up bleeding heads," Papa always said, and I couldn't agree more.

After Mrs. Parker's cherry pie, the best part of the evening was talking to Papa. He had the most interesting way of looking at things.

"Papa," I said one evening, finishing up the last crumbs of my pie. "Mrs. Parker is complaining that she can't find any decent help because all the young girls want to take factory jobs."

Papa leaned back in his chair and lit his pipe and puffed.

"Well, Janey, dignity is very important. Maybe some of these girls don't think it's very dignified washing someone else's laundry and emptying other people's chamber pots. What do you think? Would you rather work in a factory or empty chamber pots?" he asked.

It made me think, an activity Papa encouraged. "Speak up, Janey; say what's on your mind," Papa always said.

"I don't imagine it would be very nice to empty chamber pots," I admitted. But I didn't think the factory would be very nice either. The women who worked in factories had swollen ankles from standing on their feet all day.

Papa brought home books from the Library Company, where he was a member, and we read them together after supper. My favorite story was "Rip Van Winkle" by Mr. Washington Irving. Rip Van Winkle drinks too much liquor, falls asleep under a tree, and wakes up twenty years later. Rip Van Winkle greatly resembled the men of Philadelphia who spent their evenings drinking at taverns until they were senseless. It seemed a very silly activity.

"Papa," I asked. "Why are men always drinking too much liquor and getting into trouble?"

"It is a great mystery, Janey. But"—and here Papa grinned— "it keeps your poor pa in business."

And he was right, because sure enough, every evening after the taverns had closed, I'd be woken by some drunken fool roaring that he was bleeding to death on our front porch and would the good doctor please come out and sew him up?

Papa would let me get up and help him, and when we were

finished he would make me a glass of warm milk and honey and tuck me into bed.

"Where is my favorite daughter?" he would say, tweaking the end of my nose.

"She is right here. And she is your only daughter," I would say with a sleepy smile, sinking into my soft, warm bed. Then I would close my eyes and dream of the sea and Mrs. Parker's cherry pie.

Truly I was the luckiest girl in the world.

Then my luck changed. Here is how it happened.

Jebediah was Mrs. Parker's boy and my favorite playmate. He was very clever and instructed me in all manner of useful things, such as how to throw clumps of manure at passing carriages, how to tease the butcher's dog without being bitten, and how to spit. I am not boasting when I say I was excellent at spitting, the best in the neighborhood.

"You're better than the pigeons themselves!" Jebediah would say, awestruck at my ability to hit a gentleman's hat from the roof without the man even noticing. There were fellows who walked around Philadelphia all day who didn't even know that they had great gobs of spit on their hats.

Jebediah was a fine spitter himself, and quite adept at using the space where his two front teeth used to be to lob a fine one at passersby. He'd lost his two front teeth when he'd slipped on a pat of manure and hit a cobblestone. Papa said that while spitting was a handy skill, the teeth would likely not grow back.

The streets of Philadelphia were our playground. And how

we played! We played with the newspaper boys, and the orphans, and the stray dogs, and Papa said we should, if at all possible, be careful to avoid the alleys where people were dying from cholera. One of our favorite games was lobbing rotten apples at the old tree outside the Biddle house on Arch Street. It was a towering tree that seemed to reach to heaven itself, and we would spend hours trying to see who could hit the highest branch.

One autumn day Jebediah and I were challenged to a throwing contest by two boys from Arch Street, Horace Fink and Godfrey Hale. I am afraid that Horace was a disagreeable boy with big ears, and Godfrey Hale had a weepy eye and liked to stick his finger up his nose as if digging for gold.

"Me first," Horace Fink declared, snatching up an apple.

He waited for a passing carriage to go by and then threw. The apple just skimmed the trunk of the tree.

"Even Jane can do better than that," Jebediah sniffed. He handed me a particularly rotten specimen of an apple.

Horace Fink smirked at me. "You couldn't hit a stone wall."

Jebediah rolled his eyes as if to say that Horace Fink was as thick as the tree he had missed.

"Go on then," Godfrey Hale taunted.

The sun was shining brightly, the air still, the rotten apple heavy in my hand. I looked at Horace Fink's smirking face. What was I to do? Really, did I even have a choice?

Certainly not.

I wound up and threw as hard as I could. And as the apple left my hand, Sally Biddle stepped out of her house.

Need I tell you that Sally was everything that I was not? She was thirteen and perfect in all respects. Her waist was thin as a ribbon, her golden hair always styled in ringlet curls to perfection, and her skin white as milk. She was as stiff and neat as her crisp petticoats.

Time seemed to stand still, appalled, as my apple went flying through the air. It missed the tree completely and smashed square onto the bosom of Sally Biddle's pale rose dress.

I froze.

Then Sally Biddle let loose a scream so loud that windows up and down Arch Street shuddered and shook.

Horace Fink hooted with laughter. "Bully for Jane!" he shouted.

Across the street Sally Biddle was left in no doubt as to the identity of the guilty party.

"Jane Peck!" she hissed, eyes flashing.

And that was the beginning of my bad luck.

Five years later, as I sailed aboard a brig named the *Lady Luck*, it seemed bad luck was something I would never escape.

You see, when I'd dreamed of my sixteenth birthday, I had pictured an afternoon tea with girls in lovely gowns, flowers everywhere, and perhaps even one of Mrs. Parker's cherry pies. It's fair to say I'd never imagined being stuck in a tiny airless cabin, the same cabin that had been home for months on end. Instead of flowers and pie, I had a hard, narrow bunk, a rickety table and chairs, and a tiny window that wouldn't open (a most helpful feature).

At the beginning of the voyage, I had attempted to make the cabin comfortable. I'd put a linen tablecloth on the table and set embroidered cushions on the chairs. I'd laid out new china, placed a crystal vase on a small shelf, and hung a mirror on the wall.

Samuel, the cabin boy, had come by and looked around, dumbstruck.

"You sure you want to be putting all that out?" he'd asked.

That first night at sea, we sailed into a storm. Need I describe the horror that followed? The tablecloth slipped off, the cushions bounced about, the china shattered into a million pieces, and the mirror came crashing down. My companion, Mary, caught the crystal vase as it fell, and I later packed it away in my camphor wood chest along with the cushions and tablecloth. But the broken mirror had seemed a bad omen.

In the place where the mirror had hung, Mary pegged up a piece of paper with two columns. The left column said "Days at Sea," and the right said "Fleas Killed." The cabin was absolutely bursting with fleas. No matter that we shook out our blankets every day and killed as many of the pests as possible—they multiplied with staggering speed.

On the day of my birthday, I lay all morning on that hard wooden bunk, nearly unable to stand from seasickness. By noon I was no better. The ship hit a wave, and Mary groaned from her bunk on the other side of the cabin. She was nearly as sick as I.

"Happy birthday, Jane my girl," she said in her thick Irish brogue. Her face was ashen, and her black hair looked decidedly dull.

"I expect Sally Biddle didn't spend her sixteenth birthday with her head over a bucket," I said, a miserable expression on my face.

"No, but just thinking about that girl makes me want to puke," Mary said loyally, a spark lighting her dark eyes.

I smiled weakly.

The ship rolled hard, and her arm struck the bunk. She winced.

"How is your arm?" I asked.

Days earlier, I had awakened in the middle of the night to Mary's screams. Among the assorted vermin on board was a surfeit of rats, who sauntered about as bold as you please. A big, fat fellow had bitten her and then scurried off into a hole in the wall, his wormy pink tail slithering out of sight behind him.

Mary held up her arm with a grimace. Yellow pus leaked through the bandages. "I'd better change that," I said, and stood up, but before I could take a step, the ship hit a rolling wave. My belly heaved. I leaped for the bucket and sat down hard in a chair.

At that most inconvenient moment, Father Joseph banged on our cabin door.

"Mesdemoiselles," he called.

Mary groaned from the bunk and pulled the covers over her head.

Father Joseph was a French Catholic missionary. While Mary and I had spent most of the voyage being sick, he had spent most of it preaching, no doubt to be in good form to convert the savages we would find at the end of our journey. We tried to be polite to him, but Father Joseph did try one's nerves.

"Come in," I called. As he entered I reluctantly gestured to the other chair, sliding the reeking bucket under the table with my foot.

"And how does this day find you, Mademoiselle Peck?"

"Tolerably well," I replied. Tolerably well, if you considered being seasick and killing fleas respectable pursuits for a young lady on her sixteenth birthday.

"I am here to talk to you about the savages," he announced, eyes shining. Father Joseph wore a thick, black wool robe and collar, and his head was as bald as an egg. He had huge, hairy eyebrows that perched atop his eyes like fuzzy caterpillars. When he was excited, his eyebrows danced around most alarmingly.

"Not the blasted savages again," Mary whispered from beneath her blankets, and even I groaned inwardly. It was his favorite sermon, and he had preached it at least twice a week since leaving port. I could practically preach it myself by now.

"It is our Christian duty to show the savages the way of Christ," Father Joseph began, waving his arms in swooping gestures. "For they are the most unfortunate of God's creatures," he declared.

I murmured sympathetically. Privately I considered us more unfortunate than the savages. At least *they* were on dry land.

Father Joseph's eyebrows were twitching.

"Death can come at any time! The kingdom of heaven is open only to those who do God's will," he thundered, banging his fist on our rickety table for emphasis. It shuddered.

"Father," I said. "The table."

From the bunk Mary moaned dramatically. "I think I'm gonna puke," she said loudly, and groaned again.

Father Joseph eyed Mary's bunk warily.

"Perhaps we can continue this some other time," I suggested helpfully.

"But mademoiselle . . ." He hesitated.

"Pass me the bucket, Jane my girl." Mary groaned even louder. She started making retching noises.

Father Joseph looked nervously at Mary's bunk and quickly stood up. "Another time then, mesdemoiselles," he said, and made a hasty exit.

The door slammed shut.

Mary's black-haired head popped up from beneath the covers.

"Good riddance," she laughed, her eyes merry. "I've heard some of the lads say the church shipped him out so they didn't have to listen to his preaching!"

"That's not a very charitable thing to say," I admonished, but laughed. Mary was so naughty sometimes.

Mary shook her head, which sent her curls flying. "I feel sorry for the savages. He'll bore them to death before he even converts the first of them!"

Mary was not much given to good manners, but I had hope for her. Look how far I had come.

But then, I'd had considerable motivation.

You see, from the day my apple had made its acquaintance with her bodice, Sally Biddle had considered it her sovereign duty to torment me.

One late autumn afternoon had found Jebediah and me playing in the street. We were tossing manure at the backs of carriages.

"Jane, you really should use the fresh pats. They stick better,"

Jebediah suggested helpfully, flinging one at a passing carriage to demonstrate.

Just then Sally Biddle came sauntering down the cobblestone street, a gaggle of girls in her wake.

"It's a disgrace the way you're always running around with scabby boys," Sally Biddle sniffed, tossing her blond hair. Her corkscrew curls stood out like a pack of little pigs' tails all in a row. "An eleven-year-old really ought to know better."

I eyed Jebediah's knees. Come to think of it, they were scabby.

"Just look at yourself," Sally continued. "No wonder all the mothers keep their daughters from you!"

The girls gave little nods of agreement.

I looked down at myself, wondering what she meant. It was true my apron had a cherry stain on it, but this was no different from any other day. And perhaps my hair was a bit tangled and my nails were a bit stained, though that was to be expected when handling manure pats.

All the mothers kept their daughters away from me? It had never occurred to me to wonder why the other girls never played with me. After all, I had Papa and Jebediah.

"What do you mean?" I asked.

But Sally Biddle ignored me and turned to the girls.

"My mother says it's a shame that Dr. Peck has never remarried, but that it's perfectly understandable. After all, what respectable lady would want to deal with a girl like Jane? It would be like bringing a street urchin into your home." She spoke conversationally, as if she were discussing the weather or a new bonnet.

I suddenly remembered all the times I'd come home late for

supper, tracking manure from the street. How Papa would sometimes look at me and shake his head and sigh heavily. Was he secretly ashamed of me? Was I truly a disgrace? A cold, sick feeling curled in my belly.

The corners of Sally's mouth turned up in a small smile, and the sight of that knowing smile made my back stiffen. The words tumbled from my mouth in a rush.

"Papa loved my mother!" I blurted. "He's never cared for another woman!"

Sally turned on me smoothly, not a petticoat out of order, not a bow out of place. "Then he must not care for *you* very much." She paused, drawing the moment out. "After all, you're the reason she's dead!"

I stumbled back as if I'd been punched hard in the belly, the air going out of me in a rush, leaving my knees wobbly.

The other girls looked at Sally and laughed uncomfortably.

"She probably died from the shame of having a girl like you!" Sally added, and burst into peals of laughter.

I couldn't bear to hear any more.

I turned and ran.

Sally Biddle was relentless.

On an exceptionally mild February afternoon in the year 1850, I was sitting on the front step of our house on Walnut Street eating a piece of Mrs. Parker's cherry pie. Suddenly Sally Biddle appeared, like a mosquito scenting a plump, bare leg. Cora Fletcher was with her. Cora was an almost perfect replica of Sally, right down to her rabbit fur muff.

"Everyone knows that all the best people live on Arch Street," Sally Biddle remarked to Cora, as if I weren't sitting right there.

I paused, fork to my lips.

"Take this house, for instance," she said. "Why, it looks older than our stables." Sally Biddle's eyes slid up and down our house with barely concealed contempt.

I looked at our house as if for the first time.

How small and shabby it appeared! The front door needed painting, and the shutter near my bedroom window was nearly falling off from the time I had tried to climb down it. And why, our house was only two stories, instead of three stories like the houses on either side! How had I never noticed these things before? The pie in my mouth abruptly tasted sour.

Sally Biddle's eyes shined at the expression on my face.

It seemed in that moment that my entire life was a sham. I was a disgrace to my papa, I had killed my own mother, and our house was poor. I felt tears well up in my eyes.

"I declare I have never seen so fine a house in all of Philadelphia," a voice broke in.

Standing next to our gate, the buttery late afternoon sun lighting his pale blond hair like a halo, was a young man holding a leather satchel.

Sally Biddle gaped at him. Cora Fletcher gaped at him.

I gaped at him.

With his beautiful gray eyes and chiseled chin, he was hard not to gape at.

"I'm William Baldt," my hero said, tipping his hat. "And that's a nice piece of pie you have there."

* * *

Was there ever a young man such as William Baldt?

How to describe his perfection? His gray eyes, deep and wise. His lovely eyelashes, thick as a girl's, and his hair, golden and smooth, like spun wheat. Then there was his elegant nose, straight as a rail. Not to mention he had all of his teeth, front and back! And did I remark upon his ears? The perfect shape of each pink lobe?

William had come to live with us and apprentice to my father. He stayed in the spare bedroom at the back of the house and took supper with us each evening. There had been other young men who had apprenticed to my father in the past, but never one so handsome or fine or with such a charming chin.

"A promising young man, William," Papa said in an approving voice. "Nineteen and already finished medical school."

What else can I tell you about him? He was the youngest son of a large family, and a proper gentleman. He always scraped his shoes before coming into the house, and he had beautiful manners. Why, he never belched at the table or spit tobacco like the men in the taverns.

And he was kind, so very kind to me, that it was like a balm after all the terrible months of Sally Biddle. Everything seemed manageable when William was present.

One morning when I was sitting on our front step, William came out of the house. "What excitement are you up to today, Miss Peck?" he asked.

I shrugged. Most likely I would be spitting from the roof at passing gentlemen with Jebediah Parker, but I thought it best not to say anything. A man who didn't belch at the table was unlikely to approve of spitting.

A lady and gentleman came walking by. The lady looked at my stained apron and tangled hair and shook her head, pursing her lips slightly. William looked away quickly, reddening.

When they were out of sight, William gave me a measured look.

"Is that young lady still being unkind to you?" he asked.

"You mean Sally Biddle?"

"Jane," he said in a firm voice. "Perhaps if you were more . . . how do I say this? If you were more ladylike they would not be so terrible to you."

I looked at him in surprise.

"I know it's been hard because you have no mother. But you must learn how to be a proper young lady, Jane," he said, gazing at my stained apron. "One's position in Society is very important."

"But how do I learn?" My mind was whirling. You could learn such a thing? To be a proper young lady? This would solve all my troubles forever!

My hero scratched his head. "Surely there must be a girls' school around here."

I considered this for a moment.

"But if I go to school, who will help Papa with the patients?"

"A young girl like you ought not to be following her father when he is treating patients. It is most improper," he said sternly.

"But you are too big to sit on a man's belly!" I insisted.

"Whyever would I sit on some man's belly?"

"Papa says men behave better when he sets broken bones if I sit on their bellies, and that they think twice about getting into another bar brawl," I explained.

William looked very much like he wanted to laugh but didn't. Instead he said, "Jane, I have two younger sisters, and they both went to school and turned out very well. I know you could be a perfect young lady if only you would try."

"You do?" I asked, hope beating in my stomach.

"Yes, Jane," he said, his beautiful gray eyes looking deep into mine. How long his lashes were! "I do."

The very next morning I arose early, from anticipation. I selected a fresh apron, if not free of stains, at least as clean as Mrs. Parker could get it with boiling. I did my best to pull a brush through my hair and tie it in a braid.

Then, walking a safe distance behind, I followed Sally Biddle and the other girls as they made their way down Arch Street to a tidy-looking brick house. They disappeared behind a green door with a shiny brass knocker. A discreet sign hanging from the side of the door announced the name of the establishment:

MISS HEPPLEWHITE'S
YOUNG LADIES ACADEMY

I nearly lost my nerve when I saw that sign, but then I remembered William's encouraging words. I took a deep breath and walked up and knocked on the brass knocker. The sound echoed in my ears like a taunt, and my heart thumped fast.

A young, harried-looking maid answered the door.

"Yes?" she asked.

"I'm here to see Miss Hepplewhite," I said in a nervous rush.

"Do you have an appointment?"

"No," I whispered.

She looked me over and sniffed as if to say she was hardly surprised that a girl like me didn't have an appointment. She held out her hand. "Your card, please."

"Card?"

"Your calling card. You do have one, don't you?"

"No," I said, feeling as if I'd failed some important test. I didn't even know I was supposed to have a calling card.

The maid shook her head at me in a disappointed way. "What's your name?"

"Jane Peck."

She disappeared back inside the door and reappeared a moment later. "Follow me, Miss Peck."

I followed the maid down a long, cool, shadowed hallway to a closed door. She told me to sit on a chair. Miss Hepplewhite would be with me shortly.

A moment later a smooth voice called, "Come in."

I opened the door nervously.

A trim-looking older woman wearing a gray silk dress was seated behind a desk, her dark brown hair bundled discreetly in a snood, her hands clasped in front of her, all efficiency. She looked as neat as a calico print.

"Yes?" she asked, a frown wrinkling her forehead.

"Are you Miss Hepplewhite?"

"I am. How may I help you?"

I swallowed hard. "I'm Jane Peck, and I'd like to go to your school." As an afterthought, I whispered, "Please."

Miss Hepplewhite sized me up where I stood as if I were a ham she was deciding whether or not to purchase.

"How old are you?" she asked finally.

"Eleven. I'll be twelve next month," I whispered.

Miss Hepplewhite shook her head. "It is my opinion that a girl should begin her education at a young age—nine at the very latest. You are too old. Surely your mother knows this," she said in a disapproving voice.

"But I don't have a mother!" I cried.

Miss Hepplewhite went still, her face softening slightly. "Yes, of course. You are Dr. Peck's daughter, are you not?"

I nodded.

"I don't think—" she began.

"Please!" I pleaded. "I have to be a proper young lady. Otherwise my father will never marry, and it will be all my fault because I'm a disgrace!"

She studied me. "Have you had any education at all?"

"I can read and write. I went to common school until I was ten!"

Miss Hepplewhite hesitated. "Very well. I shall take you on as a special pupil." She paused, fixing me with a serious look. "But you must promise to work very hard."

I nodded furiously. I would promise anything!

"It's settled then. I'll expect you here tomorrow morning promptly at eight o'clock. Please have your father call on me to discuss the fees." Then she looked down at her writing, dismissing me.

I started toward the door.

Miss Hepplewhite paused, pen in hand, and looked up at me. "One other thing, Miss Peck."

"Yes, ma'am?"

"A clean apron tomorrow, Miss Peck. No jam stains, understood?"

"It's cherry pie, Miss Hepplewhite," I said.

She blinked. "No cherry pie stains then, Miss Peck."

"Yes, ma'am. No cherry pie."

I didn't mind if it meant forgoing cherry pie forever.

After all, I would be attending Miss Hepplewhite's Young Ladies Academy!

CHAPTER TWO
or,
Listening Well

Miss Hepplewhite's was a whole new world.

There was so much of importance to learn! We studied Etiquette, Embroidery, Watercolors, Drawing, and Music. The older girls also studied French Conversation, which Miss Hepplewhite said was crucial to a young lady's education. I had never heard anyone speak French except the baker, who would curse in it when a stray dog stole his bread, but all the girls seemed to agree with Miss Hepplewhite on this matter.

There were twelve students, and Miss Hepplewhite gave us lessons in the parlor room. The older girls sat in the back, but I sat in the front with the nine- and ten-year-olds, even though I was eleven. Sally Biddle, who was thirteen, sat in the very back. Sometimes I felt her eyes pressing into the back of my head, hot as embers, as if she were just waiting to burn me.

Miss Hepplewhite gave me a book called *The Young Lady's Confidante.*

"Consider this your bible, Miss Peck. Refer to it often," she urged, holding the small, brown-covered book as if it were a great treasure.

I turned the pages carefully.

"Please turn to Chapter Five or, Listening Well," Miss Hepplewhite instructed the class. I had already missed the first four chapters as I had joined late in the term.

She walked slowly in front of the room, her feet barely making a sound, her dove-gray petticoats swishing back and forth, soothing as a swing. The pocket watch hanging from her waist by a chain swayed slightly in time with her movements.

"A young woman should always listen well. No matter whether you are at church, on the street, or in your very own parlor, it is most important to listen carefully and quietly."

Miss Hepplewhite paused for emphasis.

"If you *listen well*, you shall always do well," she predicted.

Miss Hepplewhite suggested that we practice Listening Well as our study assignment. When someone said something clever, we were to laugh at the appropriate moment, or perhaps nod if the subject turned grave.

That evening supper was very quiet as I was so busy listening. Papa and William were discussing a case Papa was concerned about, an old banker whose toes looked rotten.

"I expect we'll have to take the foot off," Papa said with a sigh.

William disagreed. "The recommended therapy is to bleed the patient first."

"Bloodletting has taken more lives than any war," Papa

scoffed. "The man's going to lose enough blood when I remove the foot. I won't have him lose any more because of quackery." Papa was something of a radical in his profession.

"That is your opinion, of course," William said stiffly.

I very much wanted to announce that I once saw Papa lop off the rotten toes of a man who'd had a brick dropped on them, but I forced myself to listen well. I tried to nod and smile, but I am afraid that my smile looked more like a wince. And after a while my neck ached from all the nodding.

"Good heavens, girl," Papa suddenly declared. "Is there something wrong with your head? And why do you keep grimacing at us?"

Was I to smile or nod at his remark? I couldn't tell.

"Speak up, Janey," Papa said. "Why aren't you talking?"

"I'm supposed to listen well. That's what Miss Hepplewhite said."

I looked over at William for help, but he was in the middle of a coughing fit. He had the napkin at his mouth and was making a gurgling noise.

Papa roared with laughter so loud that the chandelier shook.

"Janey," he said, "is this school I'm sending you to going to turn you into one of those useless women who care for nothing but dresses?"

"I'm trying to be a proper young lady, Papa," I said in a small voice. Papa didn't understand anything!

"A worthy goal," William said, nodding his head approvingly.

Papa's eyes narrowed slightly.

"You'll be a lady in no time at all," William added. "All that is required is dedication and single-mindedness."

"Do you truly think so?" I asked shyly.

"Why, yes, I do," he said, ignoring Papa's loud snort of disdain.

A reluctant smile tugged at William's lips. When he smiled like that I had a warm feeling in my belly, nearly the same feeling I had after eating Mrs. Parker's cherry pie.

I grinned at Papa.

"Since you mentioned it, Papa, I do need new dresses. Miss Hepplewhite says mine are most unsuitable because of all the cherry stains."

Papa sighed heavily and sank back into his chair.

There was much to learn at the Young Ladies Academy, and Miss Hepplewhite considered me a challenge.

"Raw clay, that's what you are, my dear," she said, not unkindly. "But we will mold you yet."

Miss Hepplewhite demonstrated with a footstool how to enter and descend a carriage properly, which didn't involve leaping as Jebediah and I usually did.

"Like so," she said, holding up her petticoats carefully and arching one tiny foot.

She showed me how to stand gracefully, how to walk, and how to sit. I was amazed to discover that I had been standing, walking, and sitting the wrong way all these years!

Really, I didn't know anything at all!

"A young lady," Miss Hepplewhite emphasized, gazing at me, "should never skip or jump or scream."

My hand crept up timidly. "What about running?"

Miss Hepplewhite looked pained.

"Miss Peck," she said at last, "a young lady should never, ever, under *any* circumstances whatsoever, run. Should you find yourself in a situation where you are at risk, it is always preferable to faint. Do you understand me?"

The other girls giggled.

"Yes, Miss Hepplewhite," I whispered.

I knew better than to ask about spitting or lobbing manure.

How I learned! Each day I reported back to William on my successes at Miss Hepplewhite's. He alone seemed to appreciate my diligent study.

"Today we learned Chapter Seven or, Deportment at the Dinner Table. I learned that a young lady should speak in low tones, never laugh out loud, yawn, or blow her nose at the table," I informed him. "Or spit!" I added, remembering.

William was sitting at the desk in his bedroom with maps spread out in front of him.

"Really?" he asked in a distracted voice. "No spitting?"

"No belching either. Papa is going to be upset about that one."

"Hmmm," William said, his attention fixed firmly on the maps before him.

"What are those?" I asked, scrambling around the desk, trying to get a closer look.

He regarded me with serious eyes.

"Those, Miss Peck, are maps of the frontier."

"Where the Indians live?" I gasped. There were always thrilling stories about Indians in the newspapers, how they abducted women and ate babies and did all sorts of horrible things to the poor pioneers. Jebediah always said that he would like to meet some Indians one day, as long as they didn't cut off his scalp.

William nodded. "Yes, there may be savages there. You see, Jane, when I've finished my apprenticeship with your father, I'm going to go out there and make my fortune."

"Are you going to dig up gold in California?" Jebediah had told me all about his plans to go to California and dig up the gold in the ground. Jebediah had lots of big plans. I heard all about them as I practiced Listening Well.

"Not California, Jane. Every fool from Boston to the Carolinas is rushing out to dig up California. Not I. I'm not going to spend my life digging in a pit. I'm going where there's land to be had."

"Where is that?"

He pointed to a spot on the top left-hand corner of the map. "Oregon country," he said, his eyes glowing.

"Why don't you get land here, in Philadelphia?"

William laughed grimly. "I am the youngest son of five boys. There is no money left for me."

"Why not?"

"If I had been born first, my father's printing business would be mine. But I had the bad luck to be born last."

"Papa says you make your own luck," I said.

William made a dismissive sound. "Your father has many peculiar ideas. You cannot change luck. Nothing will alter the fact that my eldest brother is heir to everything." His voice softened. "And I am the heir to nothing."

"That's not fair."

"No," he murmured. "It isn't."

I wanted to say that I would give him anything to take that sad look off his face, but I remained silent.

He seemed to gather himself. "Which is why I must work twice as hard and be very clever. It is only through my own cleverness and determination that I shall succeed," he said in a firm voice.

"Like me!" I said. "I have to work hard, too. Why, I haven't thrown manure in over two months!"

But William appeared not to be listening to me. "I will have my experience as a surgeon to support me as I try to obtain land. And there is land to be had, Jane."

"What good is land?"

"Land," he said, slapping the map, "is the key to a man's fortune."

"I could go, too," I said eagerly. "I could help you."

"What would you do?" he asked, raising a smooth eyebrow.

"I could learn how to bake Mrs. Parker's cherry pie!"

"Perhaps you could, Jane," he said with a slight smile. "Perhaps you could."

The day was warm and Miss Hepplewhite's soothing voice rose comfortingly in the room. She was teaching us Chapter Eight or, Dress as a Test of Character.

"Your true character is shown in your dress, girls," she said.

A young lady should have neat habits, she explained. This meant wearing a pressed dress, a tidy bonnet, fresh petticoats and stockings, and clean gloves. Most important of all were the clean gloves. A real lady never went without clean gloves.

"Furthermore, a proper young lady must strive always to be appropriately dressed," Miss Hepplewhite said, eyeing our outfits as she walked up and down the rows. Papa had recently bought me some clothes, and I was wearing my new ensemble—a pale blue silk dress with a puff of muslin about the wrists, a new bonnet, and matching gloves. I liked it very much, but it was nothing compared to what Sally Biddle was wearing.

As usual Sally was wearing a dress of the very latest fashion. It was pink and white organdy with layers of scalloped flounces of lace ringing the skirt and caught up in small bouquets. She had added a straw bonnet trimmed with white flowers and a thickly fringed white parasol with more flowers. With all the flounces and flowers, she greatly resembled an iced cake. Everyone agreed that Sally Biddle was the best-dressed girl in the class.

And she knew it.

Sally Biddle sat up straighter as Miss Hepplewhite passed, a small, confident smile on her face. But Miss Hepplewhite continued down the row and, to my amazement, paused next to me.

"Miss Peck is a sterling example. She is wearing a simple, tasteful frock and she has taken the time to match her bonnet and gloves to it. The most elaborate dresses rarely produce the best effect. Simple outfits with thoughtful details such as muslin about the wrists are always in good taste because they allow one's true beauty to be perceived."

Sally Biddle seemed to stiffen.

"Those are lovely gloves." Miss Hepplewhite smiled approvingly. "Well done, Miss Peck."

I glowed at her praise. It was the first real praise Miss Hepplewhite had ever given me. The girls sitting around me dutifully murmured soft compliments.

Sally Biddle and some of the other girls lingered in the hall after class. I paused to listen to what they were discussing.

"It requires more than new gloves to be part of Society, wouldn't you agree, Cora?" Sally asked conversationally.

"Oh yes," Cora agreed emphatically. "After all, they let just *anyone* buy gloves."

I looked down at my new gloves, a hot, sick feeling rising in my throat.

Sally's eyes slid to mine. "Why, even my maid wears gloves, but that doesn't mean I'd ask her to tea!"

"Except perhaps to serve it!" Cora squealed.

I pushed past Sally before the tears spilled out.

Her soft laugh followed me.

I rushed down the cobblestone streets, my stomach one thick knot of shame, my eyes clouded with tears. And, of course, at this most fortuitous moment, I tripped on a fresh pat of manure, my feet going out from under me. I fell to my knees, stopping my fall with my gloved hands. As I picked myself up, people stopped and stared.

I ran the rest of the way home, crying in earnest.

"Miss Peck, whatever is the matter?" a voice said.

It was William.

Hastily I wiped my eyes.

"I'll never be part of Society!" I hiccuped.

William pulled out a pocket-handkerchief and pressed it into my hand.

I blew my nose hard, as if I could blow away all the horrible things that had happened today.

"Now tell me why you'll never be a part of Society," he said.

"My gloves!" I said, holding out my soiled hands.

"Your gloves?" he asked in a perplexed voice, recoiling slightly. They did smell awful.

"I thought that if I looked like a proper young lady, I would *be* one. But Sally Biddle said that just because you wear nice gloves, it doesn't mean you're part of Society! What if she's right? What if I never fit in?"

William was silent for a moment, as if deep in thought. Finally he said, "Jane, we are alike, you and I. It is only through our own cleverness and hard work that we will succeed. You must not allow impediments to stand in your way. You must reach for what you desire, for it will never be freely given to you. Do you understand?"

"I think so," I said finally.

William looked thoughtful. "I imagine this Sally Biddle is simply jealous of you."

"Jealous? Of me?"

"One of my younger sisters, Elizabeth, who is your age, had a similar problem with a girl like your Miss Biddle. Do you know what she did?"

"What?"

"Beth ignored her. And after a time the girl stopped taunting her." He patted my hand. "Perhaps you should ignore Miss Biddle."

The next morning Sally Biddle was in the hallway with Cora Fletcher and some other girls, waiting for class to begin.

"Keeping your gloves clean, Jane?" Sally asked brightly. "I understand Jane had a slight mishap on the way home yesterday," she explained helpfully to her audience.

The other girls looked expectantly at me. I started to feel that familiar sick feeling in my belly, but then I remembered William's good advice. I tugged up my gloves, looked straight ahead, and walked right by her and into the classroom.

"Well done," a girl seated in front of me whispered in an admiring voice.

I could not resist a peek behind me.

Sally Biddle was still standing there, staring after me like a dog who has had its bone taken away.

Miss Hepplewhite had said that Thinking and Sewing (Chapter Six) was a useful exercise, especially when one was worried or upset. And that was exactly what I was doing. For in spite of having successfully ignored Sally Biddle, I had new worries. Specifically, my waist.

An ideal young lady, Miss Hepplewhite had stressed, should have a slender waist, sunken cheekbones, and a pale face—should look, in fact, as if she were on the verge of fainting. While I might have been plump, I had never considered myself fat. Now I spent hours in front of the mirror, worrying that perhaps Mrs. Parker's cherry pies had something to do with the way my skirt pulled tight against my belly.

"You just have stout bones, Janey," Papa said, and although he was a surgeon and qualified to give an anatomical opinion, I knew he was only being kind. There was no escaping it.

I was simply enormous.

And that was the very reason I was sewing so furiously. I needed to keep my hands busy so that they wouldn't reach out for Mrs. Parker's cherry pie, waiting on the table, piping hot from the oven and smelling so tempting. Papa and William were eating it right across the room from me. I could almost taste the warm golden crust, the sweet cherries, and the thick cream dribbled over it. My stomach growled loudly as if it, too, knew that Mrs. Parker's pie was in the vicinity. Papa raised a questioning eyebrow, and I looked down quickly.

My fingers moved faster over the piece of embroidery I was sewing, a small red cherry, and I tried not to think of the way the cherries would ooze out of the pastry, tasting sweet and warm. Sewing was the one thing that Miss Hepplewhite didn't have to teach me. Papa had taught me how to sew years ago. "So you can help me stitch up cracked skulls," he said.

"Certainly is quiet living with a young lady," Papa said, looking over at me, a little sadly it seemed.

I would have responded that a lady was supposed to be quiet, but I was feeling very short of breath. I had just put on my new corset, and it was giving me considerable trouble. Trouble, in particular, with breathing. The corset was reinforced with whalebone stays, and it had taken Mrs. Parker the better part of an hour to secure it tightly at my waist. Now it felt as if a million fingers were poking into my middle. I could barely breathe. But what other option did I have? I would never have a waist as slender and ladylike as Sally Biddle's unless I did something about it. Still, I couldn't help but stare longingly at the half-embroidered cherry, imagining it peeking from a piece of flaky crust.

"Why anyone would choose to be a lady is beyond me," Papa said, addressing no one in particular. "It isn't much of a choice. Unless you like letting your brain rot and your tongue drop out from lack of good use."

I gave a ragged breath, wincing at the tightness in my middle. A thought suddenly occurred to me. This is what it must have felt like to be one of Papa's patients and be sat on by a fat little girl! No wonder they always behaved afterward.

"Why are you fidgeting so?" Papa demanded. "You look like you're being tortured, girl!"

I wanted to say that I *was* being tortured but wisely said nothing. Papa had a very poor opinion of corsets, and it had been only by begging Mrs. Parker that I had managed to secure one.

"Well?" he asked again.

"I'm fine," I said.

"You're not wearing one of those corsets, are you, Janey?" he asked suspiciously. "There's nothing fashionable about crushed organs."

"Papa!" I hissed. What was Papa thinking, to discuss such things in William's presence!

"Hmmph," he said.

"Papa, I need some money," I said, eager to change the subject.

"Do you now?"

"I need to buy ribbons for my bonnet. Miss Hepplewhite says that dress is a test of character, and all the girls at Miss Hepplewhite's have ribbons on their bonnets."

Papa snorted. "What have ribbons got to do with character? Besides, I just bought you three new dresses, two parasols, a cloak, and two pairs of shoes. Not to mention four pairs of gloves. Four pairs! That's quite enough, I think, for one small girl who can't be bothered to speak her mind at the supper table."

"But Papa," I pleaded. "All the girls have ribbons!"

"Then you'll be the only ribbonless girl in Philadelphia. I'm sure you'll survive."

"But—"

"There is more to life than amassing a wardrobe. When was the last time you picked up a book?" He shook his head. "I did not raise you to be a vain and shallow girl."

"But Papa—"

"No, Janey," he said firmly. "And I don't want to hear another word."

The next afternoon William was waiting for me when I returned home from the Young Ladies Academy.

"For you," he said, placing a small, paper-wrapped packet in my hand.

I looked at him in astonishment.

"Go on," he said with a beautiful smile. Have I mentioned he had all his teeth? "Open it."

My hands trembled as I unwrapped the paper. I gasped when I saw what was inside. Beautiful green silk ribbons, more than a dozen. Enough to decorate several bonnets!

"They're beautiful," I whispered. I had never received a more precious gift in my whole life! Papa usually gave me boring gifts, never anything as wonderful and important as ribbons!

He nodded.

"I'll treasure them," I said earnestly. "They'll look lovely on my new bonnet."

"Yes," William said. "A bonnet is just the thing to tame that hair of yours."

I nodded, patting my wild hair. What a good idea.

"Green suits you, Jane," he said. "You should always wear green."

"I shall," I solemnly vowed.

It seemed that no time passed at all, but months disappeared and suddenly William's tenure with Papa was at an end.

William announced his intentions at supper one dark, winter evening. A crisp wind promising snowy days ahead drifted through the crack of an open window. I looked out a window, imagining William and me strolling down the snow-covered street, my hand resting lightly on his arm, his eyes smiling down at me.

"I have secured passage as surgeon on a clipper ship bound for San Francisco," William said, beaming. "The *Sea Witch*."

I sat up abruptly.

"You're leaving?" I asked in a stunned voice. "When?"

"Tomorrow. We leave on the tide."

"Tomorrow," I echoed dully. I remembered all his talk about wanting to go west, but still, how could he leave me?

Papa looked equally surprised but quickly gathered his wits. "Congratulations. That's a fine post. You'll get plenty of experience."

"It's a way to get west." William shrugged. "I plan to head north and settle on Shoalwater Bay, in Oregon country. The government is offering land grants to settlers."

"There can't be many pioneers out there," Papa said curiously. "Who will you treat?"

I could not believe that Papa was capable of asking such questions! Why didn't he ask William to stay on? He needed William as much as I . . . didn't he?

William inclined his head. "I shall minister to whatever pioneers are there, but I am interested in the land. And the timber on it. It is my intention to make my fortune in timber."

Papa looked taken aback.

"All that study to become a surgeon and you want to chop down trees?" Papa asked in a shocked voice.

"There's more money to be had in chopping down trees than chopping off limbs," William replied coolly.

Papa grunted. "You'll have to move a few Indians to get to the land."

"The savages shall be obliged to move," William said, completely unconcerned.

"Hard way to make a fortune if you ask me," Papa said. "Full of danger."

William pursed his lips. "I have nothing to lose."

"Except life and limb," Papa said dryly.

I coughed loudly, trying to get Papa's attention.

"You getting sick, Janey?" he asked.

I stared at Papa mutinously. Why didn't he say something to make William stay? Why was he letting him leave?

Papa turned back to William, raising his glass in a toast.

"Good luck to you, especially with the Indians," Papa said. "I suspect that'll be harder than the doctoring and timber." He sounded amused.

I put my glass to my lips but could not swallow. Nor could I eat another bite. All I could do was sit silently at my place and glare at Papa and William, furious at both heartless men. They were impossible. Could they not see I was dying inside?

After supper I went to William's room. He was packing his leather satchel. I stood watching in the doorway. His maps were already stowed away, as were the books that had littered his desk. There was not a single personal possession in sight. It was as if he had never even been here.

"Must you go?" I whispered, reaching out to put a hand on his arm.

He turned around, startled.

"I'm afraid I must," he said, regarding me with his gray eyes. When would I see those eyes again? Or those lovely eyelashes, for that matter?

"But you can't leave!" I said helplessly. "What will I do?"

"If you write to me, it will be as if I am still here," he said easily.

No it won't! I wanted to shout. A letter would never listen to me or give me advice on Sally Biddle or bring me ribbons!

"Will you promise to write me?" he asked.

"I promise," I said fervently.

"You're a good girl, Jane Peck," he said, and kissed my hand lightly.

He was gone the next morning.

CHAPTER THREE
or,
A Woman's Peculiar Calling

How I dreamed of William in the months that followed! His gray eyes and bright blond hair filled my thoughts. And, of course, his lovely teeth!

"Girls," Miss Hepplewhite declared. "Please open your books to Chapter Ten."

I looked out the window, daydreaming about William. The summer of 1851 had come and gone in its hot, hazy way, and the crisp scent of autumn was in the air. I was thirteen now, and the girl who had run around eating pies all day and playing with Jebediah Parker was a distant memory.

"Who would like to read?"

I raised my hand. Now that I was older, I sat in the middle of the room. I had made a few friends, but Sally Biddle was not one of them.

"Go on, then, Miss Peck."

I cleared my throat. By now we had reviewed each chapter of *The Young Lady's Confidante* numerous times. I almost might have recited the text from memory: "'Chapter Ten or, A Woman's Peculiar Calling. It is a woman's peculiar calling to please those around her. Do not put your own desires in the forefront, but rather think first of your good parents, your brothers and sisters, and most especially, one day, your husband.'" I looked up.

"Well done." Miss Hepplewhite paused, looking at us with serious eyes. "Girls, you must strive always to please others and do so cheerfully. For this is where your true happiness lies."

She toured the room.

"One means of obtaining this happiness is to make your house a home. By bringing cheerfulness to your home, you express your grace and refinement to those around you."

Some of the girls in front of me nodded their heads thoughtfully.

"Little details should not be overlooked," Miss Hepplewhite continued. "Fresh flowers or a thoughtfully designed menu that takes into consideration the particular tastes of your guests is a perfect example."

Miss Hepplewhite smiled and clasped her hands.

"A well-ordered home is a miniature of heaven."

Sally Biddle leaned forward. "What a shame, Jane," she murmured. "I shouldn't think any man will consider that house on Walnut Street a miniature of heaven. Although it *is* small."

My eyes started to sting. I bit my lip to keep from crying.

"Miss Biddle," Miss Hepplewhite called in a firm voice.

"Yes, Miss Hepplewhite?" Sally Biddle said politely.

"The size of one's house does not determine the nature of one's character, Miss Biddle."

Sally Biddle flushed in embarrassment.

"And Miss Biddle," Miss Hepplewhite said sternly. "A person who says unkind things is not a proper young lady."

I looked gratefully at Miss Hepplewhite.

She nodded almost imperceptibly and turned back to the lesson.

I went home inspired to prepare a meal that would please Papa. Mrs. Parker and I were discussing my idea in the kitchen when there was a knock at the front door.

"Oh dear," she said. She was covered in flour.

"I'll get it," I offered. A lady should always be cheerful and helpful!

I opened the front door and bright light flooded in. I blinked and for a brief moment my heart leaped. William? Then I blinked again. It wasn't William after all. It was just a deliveryman from Blood's Penny Post.

"Letter, miss," the man said, holding out the packet.

I gave him a coin and took the envelope, turning it over in my hands. It was rumpled and thin and a little dirty, as if it had passed through many hands to arrive at Walnut Street.

It was from William!

I ran upstairs to my bedroom and closed the door. My hand shook in excitement as I imagined what he had written. I could practically hear his words. No doubt he would say how much he missed me and our little talks and how he couldn't wait to return to Philadelphia to be with me. I tore open the envelope carefully and went to a window to read the single sheet of paper.

May 15, 1851

Dear Miss Peck,

Having arrived in relative safety at Shoalwater Bay, I am now undertaking to become better situated with my surroundings.

It is a rich countryside. Game and fish are plentiful. The local band of savages is called Chinooks. They are very skilled at trading and have been trading for many years with the British. I am told that their numbers have been much reduced by disease, but there are still many in the area.

My regards to your father.

As ever, I remain,
William Baldt

I nearly cried with disappointment.

He hadn't even inquired about me! Had I meant so little to him? The letter seemed almost impersonal. Did this mean he was actually going to stay out there? Would I never see his lovely eyes again? I stared hard at the letter and felt my throat go tight at the very thought.

"Jane, do you think I should make a plum pudding?" Mrs. Parker called up the stairs.

I swallowed hard and put the letter on my desk and hurried down to help her.

* * *

I threw myself into my studies to take my mind off William's disappointing letter.

While I enjoyed the Embroidery and Watercolors and Drawing and Music classes, Etiquette was still my favorite subject.

There was The Importance of Punctuality (Chapter Nine): "Young ladies who are not punctual when traveling think up any manner of excuses. The truth is the unpunctual do not allow themselves sufficient time," Miss Hepplewhite said, pointing to the ever-present pocket watch that hung from the chain on her skirt.

Being a Good Guest (Chapter Eleven): "A gracious guest should not interfere with the domestic routine of the house. Be as little trouble as possible. Never," Miss Hepplewhite stressed, "*never* be in the way."

And, of course, Pouring Tea and Coffee (Chapter Three): "A young lady who can preside over pouring tea and coffee shall always be admired," Miss Hepplewhite promised.

We also reviewed Rules of Conversation (Chapter Two), Receiving and Returning Calls (Chapter Four), Deportment on the Street (Chapter Thirteen), Care of Odd Minutes (Chapter Fourteen), and The Particulars of Domestic Economy (Chapter Fifteen).

Then came the fateful day when we learned about the Great Mistake.

Strangely enough, there was no chapter in *The Young Lady's Confidante* with this title.

Miss Hepplewhite looked very grave as she stood at the

front of the classroom, leaning next to her elegantly carved desk, her hands clasped in front of her.

"Dear girls," she said, her voice catching. "If you learn no other lesson from me, learn this." She lowered her eyes.

We leaned forward.

"Beware the Great Mistake."

Some older girls near the back giggled.

Miss Hepplewhite looked up sharply, and the room went quiet. The only sound was a bird singing outside the window.

"A kiss may seem innocent, but it is the greatest mistake a young woman can make, for it leads to other intimacies, and that is the path to destruction."

I remembered William's kiss on my hand. How it had tingled and felt warm for days after. How I had resolved not to wash it but had in the end, as it had become sticky with jam.

There were more giggles from the back of the room.

"Modesty, girls, that is your watchword. Do not allow a handsome face to lead you astray."

Her voice was nearly a whisper.

"Beware the Great Mistake."

After school I heard some of the older girls talking.

"The Great Mistake!" Sally Biddle mimicked. "I shouldn't mind making a few mistakes with that nice Horace Fink."

The girls giggled.

"Or Godfrey Hale," Cora Fletcher suggested in a hushed voice. "He has a very agreeable face."

And while it was true that Horace Fink and Godfrey Hale had grown up, all I could remember was Horace's big ears and Godfrey's finger up his nose.

Sally Biddle caught sight of me.

"Jane Peck," Sally Biddle said in a satisfied voice. "My, what an unusual hairstyle. Wouldn't you agree, Cora?"

"Very interesting, indeed," Cora murmured.

"Yes." Sally looked at me, an innocent expression on her face. "It reminds me of a—a—"

She paused, searching for the right words.

A squirrel scampered up a nearby oak tree.

"A squirrel's nest!" she finished, a bland expression on her face.

The girls laughed.

I touched my hair self-consciously, noticing the stray strands coming free from the knot I had arranged that morning. It wasn't my fault my hair was curly and prone to looking wild. I was doing the best I could.

And I *was* good enough. I had studied faithfully and knew how to pour tea and embroider handkerchiefs and listen well. Even Miss Hepplewhite said that I would make a fine wife, that I was pious and meek and modest in all respects.

I thought of William's letter waiting on my desk, unanswered.

"As a matter of fact, I am corresponding with a most agreeable gentleman, Dr. William Baldt," I said in a steady voice, amazing myself. "And he thinks my hair is most becoming."

"William Baldt?" Cora Fletcher asked curiously. Her eyes lit up. "I remember him! He *is* indeed a most agreeable young man."

I smiled triumphantly at Sally.

But she just narrowed her eyes.

When I returned home, I hastily penned William a reply.

October 2, 1851

Dear Dr. Baldt,

I was ever so pleased to receive your letter. Did you know that it took nearly four months to reach my hands?

This day Miss Hepplewhite discussed how to avoid draggled petticoats. The recommended way is to hold one's skirts at the back so as not to reveal one's ankles when strolling. It is very scandalous to reveal one's ankles, although Papa says there is nothing particularly scandalous about mine.

Mrs. Parker has hired a new girl. Her name is Mary Hearn, and she is Irish. Mary is two years older than I and says she doesn't care a whit if some man sees her ankle; she isn't about to kill herself tripping considering the number of times she goes up and down the stairs every blessed day.

I like her very much, even if she is a bit crude.

Could you please write me some interesting things about the wild frontier?

Yours truly,
Miss Jane Peck

Many months later I received his next letter. I ripped it open, eagerly looking for any sign of his affection for me. To my dismay, none was to be found.

January 12, 1852

Dear Miss Peck,

Thank you for your letter. I hope your studies at Miss Hepplewhite's are going well. You know my opinion on these matters.

The Donation Law grants a man 640 acres if he improves the tract. As you know, I am intent on acquiring land, so this is a very good proposition. The first thing I did upon my arrival was to choose a fine piece of land and duly stake my claim.

Regarding your request for stories of the wild frontier, truly this part of the frontier is not so very wild. We have all the comforts of home. The pioneers are engaged in a number of industries, chiefly oystering and timber.

Your letter reminded me of the lovely meals at Walnut Street. I'm sorry to say that not one of the men on Shoalwater Bay can produce meals as satisfying as Mrs. Parker's. I miss her cherry pie very much.

As ever, I remain,
William Baldt

I would have given anything for him to have written that he missed *me* and not Mrs. Parker's cherry pie. It was so disheartening. Even so, I faithfully wrote back that very day.

May 18, 1852

Dear Dr. Baldt,

I assure you that I am working very hard at Miss Hepplewhite's.

In fact, I shall relate to you the lesson I learned this very day.

Did you know that when calling on acquaintances, the visit should last no longer than ten minutes? Miss Hepplewhite related to us that a lengthy unwelcome visit is, above all, A Snare to Be Avoided. It is also vital that a return call be made no longer than a week following the first call so as not to offend. But as much visiting occurs, and in order to avoid forgetting who has visited when and whom one is obliged to visit, Miss Hepplewhite recommended keeping a list of all visitors. It is a clever idea and I have begun a list.

Miss Hepplewhite has announced an embroidery contest in school. I am going to sew a small pocket-handkerchief.

I think of you often and hope that you are thinking of me.

Yours truly,
Miss Jane Peck

Christmas arrived and with it another letter from William. It was, without question, the best of gifts!

September 1, 1852

My dearest Jane,

The arrival of a letter from Philadelphia and Miss Jane Peck is a very happy occasion on Shoalwater Bay. I'm afraid no one on the Bay possesses your wit and charm.

As it takes so long for the mail to make a round trip from Philadelphia to Shoalwater Bay, there is no need for you to wait for my letters before penning me one of your own. Therefore, I dearly hope you will be encouraged to write me whenever the fancy takes you, and I shall do the same.

It is quite apparent from your correspondence that you are becoming a most accomplished young lady. No one out here keeps with such good etiquette, but perhaps I shall recommend it.

I miss the wonderful suppers at Walnut Street. Most of all, I miss your delightful company. Do you still wear green? Please consider this ribbon a token of my special affection for you. I eagerly await your next correspondence.

You are in my thoughts and heart always.

As ever, I remain,
William Baldt

I held the slender pale green ribbon to my lips and smiled. If I had doubted that William returned my affections, I did so no longer. His most recent letter made his warm feelings clear.

William's sweet letters sustained me through the hard months of winter and rainy days of spring when it seemed that everything I accomplished at Miss Hepplewhite's disappointed Papa.

Like the day I won the embroidery contest.

It had been exciting beyond words. I had drawn top marks for my embroidery of a small violet on a pocket-handkerchief. I had even bested Sally Biddle, who had sewn a dove—a rather lopsided dove, in my opinion. Miss Hepplewhite declared that I had the neatest small stitch of any girl ever to attend the academy.

Her praise rang in my ears all the way home. I could hardly wait to tell Papa the good news.

He was sitting in his study reading a book and eating a piece of Mrs. Parker's cherry pie when I rushed in the door.

"Papa, look," I said, waving the prize handkerchief in the air. "I won! I won first prize!"

"Hmmph," he said, sounding unimpressed. "I'll be sure to have you stitch some flowers on the forehead of my next patient."

Disappointment rushed through me. Didn't he understand how important this was? I stomped my foot. "Papa!"

Papa sighed, his face gray. He was very tired of late, and I knew it was because of the yellow fever. Mothers and fathers had been banging on our door at all hours, bringing their sick children. Papa forbade me to come downstairs when patients called.

"There's no vaccination for yellow fever, Janey. I don't want you endangered."

He had kept me trapped upstairs last year too, when smallpox had raged through the slums. And there *was* a vaccination for smallpox. His excuse then had been, "Janey, the vaccination is generally effective, but there have been cases reported of vaccinated persons getting the pox, and I don't want you endangered."

Papa looked at my face and softened. "Oh Janey," he said, his voice catching. "I miss my little girl. What's happened to you? Now all I hear is talk of pouring tea and fashion and embroidery. And the only book you ever read is that useless etiquette book!"

"But Papa—"

"Here," he said in an encouraging voice. "Sit down and *talk* to me." He held out his plate. "Have a piece of pie with your dear old pa. It's Mrs. Parker's cherry pie. Your favorite."

"I can't eat pie," I said stiffly, putting my hand to the corset on my waist. While my waist was somewhat slimmer, I had a considerable way to go before I looked on the verge of fainting, as Miss Hepplewhite recommended.

"Why not?"

"Because I'm fat! I'm fat as a pig! And I'll never have a waist as thin as Sally Biddle's if I go around eating pie!" I shouted in frustration.

Papa smiled gently. "Janey," he said. "My sweet Janey. You're not fat. You're lovely. You're the picture of your beautiful mother."

"Then my mother was fat!" I burst out.

Papa went white.

I turned and ran from the study.

"Janey!" he barked.

But I just closed my bedroom door and cried.

You can see why I came to depend on William's encouraging words. He alone seemed to understand the importance of my education. And all my hard work was paying off. The proof of it arrived one warm May afternoon in a heavy, crisp envelope—an invitation to the Midsummer Gala at Cora Fletcher's house. Mr. and Mrs. Fletcher's Midsummer Gala was an annual event, and invitations were greatly coveted.

Mary and I spent all our time finding me the perfect dress and endlessly discussed how she would arrange my hair. She tried out different styles in the evenings. My favorite was a fashionable one that involved a lot of ringlet curls. I thought it was quite charming, if a little complicated.

"I think it's lovely," I said, patting the curls.

Mary just shook her head. "If ya want to look like a sheep."

When the day of the gala arrived, the house was a hive of activity with Mrs. Parker and Mary almost as excited as I was.

"What's all the fuss about?" Papa asked.

"Oh sir, our young miss is going to her first party!" Mrs. Parker said, beaming.

"Party?"

"I've been invited to Cora Fletcher's Midsummer Gala!" I said in exasperation. "I told you *weeks* ago."

"Cora who?"

"Cora *Fletcher*, Papa!"

"That Harry Fletcher's girl?"

"Yes, Papa. The Fletchers are only one of the most important families in Philadelphia!"

"Harry Fletcher important?" he asked, rubbing his beard thoughtfully.

"Papa!"

He sighed wearily and looked at me standing there in my fancy evening dress. "You look lovely," he said gruffly. "You'll be the most beautiful girl there."

When I arrived at the Fletcher house, the rooms were already full of impeccably dressed girls and handsome young men. I smoothed my pale green skirt self-consciously and checked my hair in the hall mirror.

"Hello, Jane," Cora Fletcher said. "What a charming dress."

"Thank you." I smiled nervously. "You have a lovely house."

She shrugged. "I suppose so."

I followed her into the parlor, where a group of girls were in rapt conversation. I felt a moment's anxiety. But, remembering Miss Hepplewhite's advice on such situations, I took a deep breath, pasted on a winning smile, and took a step toward them. Almost immediately I felt a tap on my shoulder.

"Would you like some punch, Jane?" Sally Biddle asked, her eyes mild, a cup in her hands.

"That would be lovely," I said, surprised but pleased, taking the cup.

Sally Biddle peered across the room. "I do believe I see Horace Fink."

And as she brushed past me I felt her arm shove my elbow

hard. The glass tipped and punch soaked the bosom of my dress and dripped down my skirts.

"Oh dear! What a mess," Cora Fletcher said, shaking her head.

The other girls eyed me with pity.

From across the room I saw Sally Biddle's grin.

The next morning the letter arrived that would change my life forever. And not a moment too soon. I had not gone to school as my eyes were puffy and swollen from crying all night.

February 14, 1853

My dearest Jane,

How time has passed. Has it truly been three years since last I saw your face? When I think of you I picture you in a beautiful green dress with your lovely red hair caught up. I miss you more than words can say.

By my calculations, you shall be past fifteen as you read this letter, and I imagine you are now an accomplished, lovely young woman.

Do you recall how you said that you would like to come out to the frontier with me one day? I am now situated in comfortable accommodations on Shoalwater Bay.

Will you, dearest Jane? Will you come west and be my wife?

As ever, I remain, your devoted servant,
William

The letter shook in my hand. William wanted to marry me? Joy rushed through me. Being his wife was the answer to all my dreams. And after last evening, I knew that there was nothing for me here in Philadelphia. Sally Biddle would always be there, waiting to ruin my happiness.

I ran to Papa's study and burst in without even knocking.

Papa looked up and rubbed his eyes. He took a small bottle of medicine and drank from it.

"Not green again," he said, eyeing my dress and rubbing his lips. "Did you make every dress out of the same god-awful bolt of fabric? I never see you in any other color."

I was determined not to lose my temper. "William says that green suits me."

Papa snorted. "If you like the color of bile."

I refused to dignify that remark with a response.

"Papa, look," I said urgently, holding out the letter.

Papa stared at the letter for a long time. When he looked up there was a shuttered expression on his face.

"No," he said.

"But Papa—"

"You're too young to be married."

"I'm fifteen!"

He slammed his fist on his desk, upsetting the little bottle.

"No daughter of mine is going out to the godforsaken frontier! There's cholera on the trail. You'll die before you even get there!"

"Then I shall take a ship!"

"You will not. You will stay here."

"But I love him!"

The room went silent.

Papa opened his mouth to speak, but all that came out was a cough. Soon he was coughing so hard that he was fighting for air, his whole body shaking. I rushed around the desk to help him.

"Papa!"

He coughed into his handkerchief and then pushed me away, his eyes watery and red.

"Don't you have school today?" he asked harshly, a bleak expression on his face. He turned his back on me and stared out the window.

Miss Hepplewhite had said that a young lady might employ tears to further her goals, but tears had little effect on my iron-willed papa.

Papa just shook his head and handed me a handkerchief.

"Janey," he said, "you are transfixed with William for the wrong reasons. There's nothing for you out on that frontier. It's dangerous. There are plenty of eligible young bachelors right here in Philadelphia. There's no call to follow one out west, especially one with no sense."

I bristled. "You're mistaken! William is the finest man with whom I have ever been acquainted."

"What kind of man throws away an education to chop down trees?" Papa demanded fiercely. "William has chosen a hard and dangerous and lonely life by settling on the frontier, a life that I don't want my only daughter to share."

"I'd rather be dead than be without William!" I said, my voice rising to a pitch.

"Janey," Papa said in a weary voice. "You are being very foolish now."

The house was in an uproar. Everyone had an opinion about the situation.

"Oh miss, it'll break the doctor's heart if you go away," Mrs. Parker said, sounding miserable.

Even Mary required convincing.

I sat at the dressing table as Mary brushed my hair with long, smooth strokes. While I had acquaintances at school, Mary was the one to whom I most often told my troubles. She was sweet and wise, and I found her company a great comfort. Not to mention she was the only one who could do anything with my hair.

"Papa is the most stubborn man in all of Philadelphia," I said, staring hard at my reflection in the mirror.

"Well, ya have the most stubborn hair in all of Philadelphia," Mary said. "It must come from somewhere."

I would not be humored out of my mood. "Papa understands nothing. Does he want me to end up a spinster? Can't he see how wonderful William is?"

"Dr. Peck seems smart enough to me," Mary said with a sharp tug to my hair.

"Ouch! Don't pull so!"

"Why would ya want ta leave?" she asked, waving a hand around my bedroom, at the four-poster bed, the quilt, the curtains.

"You couldn't possibly understand," I said.

The brush tugged my scalp painfully.

"Mary! That hurt!"

"Sorry," Mary said with an innocent grin and a half shrug. "Never learned how to brush hair. We Irish girls don't understand anything, ya know."

"Very amusing." I studied Mary in the mirror. "What about you, Mary? What do you want?"

"Well," Mary said, looking thoughtful. "I'd like something of my own. Where I'd be my own mistress. Free to do as I pleased."

She said *free* with such longing that I was startled.

"But Mary, you're as free as any young woman."

Mary stared at me and said, "Am I now? Do ya really think so, Miss Jane? I have to make a living, Jane my girl," she explained patiently. "Ya wouldn't understand."

"I'm sure there are a lot of hungry men on the frontier who would appreciate your cooking," I said.

Her eyes met mine in the mirror.

"I could have a boardinghouse. I could make a fortune," she said, her dark eyes glinting, warming to the idea. She groaned dramatically. "I'd go there just so I wouldn't have to comb this tangled mess every blessed day!"

I grabbed Mary's hand and she smiled at me.

"Would you come with me if I went out west?"

Mary grinned, her eyes bright.

"Jane my girl, what would you do without me?"

* * *

It seemed that my very strength wore on Papa, that as the weeks went by, he grew paler and thinner. Following a warm August, September arrived, and with it a dark chill that seemed to settle in my bones. Everyone was in a bad mood, especially Papa, who glared at me whenever I mentioned William's name.

One night after a particularly strained supper, someone knocked on the door. I assumed it was a patient clamoring for my father's attentions. Mary appeared at the door of the dining room with a distinguished older-looking man carrying a physician's satchel.

"Dr. Burns," she announced, tipping her dark head respectfully.

Papa stood up and shook the other man's hand. "Thank you for coming, Stanley." He turned to me. "You remember my colleague, Dr. Burns?"

"Yes, of course." He had been to the house before. Papa was always bringing people home for supper—other physicians, lawyers, bankers. Once, he even brought a judge!

"Miss Peck." Dr. Burns nodded his head gravely. He seemed a very somber sort of man.

"You must excuse us, Jane. Dr. Burns and I have some rather urgent matters that require our attention."

They locked themselves in Papa's study, and when they emerged Papa's face was gray.

The next morning he called me into his study. It was icy cold, the fire mere embers, and I wondered how long he had been sitting in the room. He stared into the fireplace, so still that he seemed almost a statue.

"Papa?"

"Janey," he said, looking up at me. His face was pink and his cheeks were rosy. He looked better than he had in weeks. Perhaps Dr. Burns had given him a tonic.

"You are looking well, Papa," I said.

He nodded simply. "You are my dearest daughter and I love you very much."

I wanted to laugh and say, "I'm your only daughter," but I was too old for such nursery games, and besides, I was angry with him for not letting me marry William.

He paused. "I have made a decision."

"A decis—"

He held up his hand to silence me. "If it means so much to you to go west and marry William, then I find I cannot stand in your way."

I could hardly believe it.

"Is this what you truly want?"

"Yes, Papa," I said quickly. "It is what I want more than anything."

"Then go," he said, his voice breaking. His eyes were wet with tears. "If it means that much to you, my dear stubborn girl, then go. You must make your own luck."

I posted William a letter accepting his offer the very next day.

When Mary and I departed two months later on the *Lady Luck*, Mrs. Parker and Papa came to the docks to bid us farewell. I stood on deck and waved to Papa as we sailed away.

And watched as he and all that I had ever known slowly disappeared.

CHAPTER FOUR
or,
Helpful Hints on Travel

I was having the most pleasant dream.

We were in the parlor on Walnut Street. A cheery fire was blazing, and Papa was reading to me from "Rip Van Winkle." The delicious aroma of Mrs. Parker's cherry pie mingled in the air with the familiar smell of Papa's pipe. It was all so warm and safe.

And then, all at once, the ship gave a sickening lurch and I awoke with a start, banging my head on the low ceiling of the cabin.

"Blast!" I shouted, rubbing my head.

"Had a pleasant nap, then, Jane my girl?" Mary asked brightly. I scowled at her.

With a huff of frustration, I pushed back the sheets and dangled my feet over the edge of the bunk and rested them on the floor. My stockings were immediately soaked through. I looked down in dismay. The bucket of seawater Samuel had brought in that morning had sloshed all over the floor.

We had been making do with cold seawater for bathing for the entire trip, and my skin was dreadfully itchy. "I do believe I'd give almost anything for a proper bath," I said fervently, scratching at my ankle in a most indelicate way.

"Ya ain't getting any argument from me on that count, Jane my girl," Mary said with a sniff.

I poured some of the dreaded seawater into the basin and stripped down to my chemise for yet another cold, salty scrubbing. My hipbones jutted sharply against the thin cotton fabric. This voyage had done more good to my waist than four years of avoiding pies. I had lost so much weight that my cheeks were sunken, and what bosoms I'd possessed had shrunk to mere bumps. I had little trouble lacing up my corset these days.

"Ya look like a scrawny lad," Mary said, disapproval clear in her voice.

"I look like a real young lady now," I countered. "Being slender and pale and having cheeks white as snow is all the fashion."

"If ya've got the consumption." Mary snorted.

"Oh Mary!"

"Are ya sure yer not contagious, Jane my girl?" she teased.

I dug through my trunk for a passably clean dress, which I was altogether unlikely to find as almost every stitch of clothing I owned was by now soiled. The very first thing I intended to do when we landed at Shoalwater Bay was launder my clothes.

As Miss Hepplewhite advised, I had packed lightly, being careful to bring only plain, neat dresses, bonnets, stockings, gloves, and plenty of handkerchiefs. But my most precious possession lay on the bottom of the trunk.

My wedding dress.

We had copied a design from *Godey's Lady's Book*. The dress was made of ivory velvet and yards and yards of lace. It had taken Mrs. Parker, Mary, and me nearly two months to make it. And when it became clear that we would miss the first ship to San Francisco I had posted William a second letter informing him of our delay. I hoped he would not be too disappointed but knew he would approve once he saw the dress. It was the most beautiful dress in the entire world. I held it to my chest and smiled.

"I surely hope this lad's worth crossing two oceans," Mary said, eyeing the dress skeptically.

I forced myself to remember William's beautiful gray eyes and his chiseled chin. "Oh Mary, he is," I replied in a steady voice.

But I felt a tingle of unease, remembering Sally Biddle's reaction.

Sally Biddle had laughed out loud when I announced my engagement.

"Engaged?" she'd mocked, her lip curling. "Dr. Baldt is clearly deluded. What lies have you been telling him in your letters? The moment he catches sight of that hair of yours he'll come to his senses." She'd smiled at me triumphantly. "And you'll wind up a spinster living among the savages!"

With a sigh I packed away my wedding finery and pulled out a plain green walking dress of cashmere edged with corded velvet ribbon. It had a rather awful stain on the bosom from where a plate with gravy had fallen on it during a particularly rough night at sea, but it was the most presentable of all my clothes.

"You know what I miss most, Mary?" I said. We often passed the time debating what we missed most. It was usually food, as the fare on board the *Lady Luck* was generally dreadful and the chief reason I had lost so much weight. We had stopped briefly to drop our cargo in San Francisco, and it was rumored we had taken on fresh provisions, but if we had, none had appeared in our cabin.

"What?"

"I would give anything for a slice of Mrs. Parker's cherry pie," I said with real longing.

"Or her biscuits and gravy," Mary said, her eyes shining.

"Or her roast pork and apples."

With a sigh, I settled down in my bunk, pulled out *The Young Lady's Confidante,* and began reading aloud to Mary as I had done over the course of the long voyage to help her better herself.

"'Chapter Three or, Pouring Tea and Coffee. A lady should always pour the first cup of tea from the pot for the youngest guest, as it is likely to be weak, and therefore most suitable for a child,'" I read. "That's a very sensible idea, don't you agree, Mary?"

She yawned.

"Miss Hepplewhite says that the way a lady pours tea and coffee is a true sign of her character," I continued.

Mary snorted. "Where's the character in pouring a bleeding cup of tea?"

That sounded suspiciously like something Papa would say.

"It requires experience and judgment and exactness to add

the perfect combination of sugar and cream to each guest's taste," I said earnestly.

"Ain't nothing special about adding sugar if yer lucky enough to have the money for it."

"Don't be obstinate, Mary. Pouring tea is the truest test of a lady. Miss Hepplewhite says that a young lady who can pour a good cup of tea will always find a husband."

"Jane my girl, I know ya mean well, but I think yer daft. Ya know what I want in a husband?"

"What?"

Mary leaned back against her pillow and stared at a spider working its way lazily across the cabin ceiling.

"I want a man who'll let me be. Someone who isn't always telling me what to do."

I stared at her.

"I'm tired of being told what to do," she said firmly. "I have a head on my shoulders, thank you very much."

"Well, my ideal is a man who brings out the best in me," I said, remembering how kind William had been to see potential in an ill-mannered girl who ran around all day with pie stains on her dress—a girl, it was plain to see, who had no sense.

"Aye, that's very agreeable," Mary said, clutching the pillow to her like a sweetheart. "When two people complement each other so perfectly." When she said it, it sounded like "pairfectly."

"If it weren't for William, I'd be a completely different sort of person," I went on.

Mary dropped the pillow. "That's not exactly what I meant, Jane my girl."

I picked up the pillow. "I owe everything to William. He's the whole reason I attended Miss Hepplewhite's."

Mary looked at me. I could tell she wasn't impressed.

"If it hadn't been for him, I would never have become a respectable young lady," I said.

We were interrupted by a knock at the door. It was Samuel, and he was holding a tray. Samuel looked no more than eleven, with wide brown eyes and a gap where his front tooth should be. He reminded me greatly of my old playmate Jebediah Parker.

"What's that?" he asked.

"This is a very important book, Samuel," I explained.

"Is that the book about the murdering white whale?" he asked excitedly. "I heard about that book there. You know, I seen whales lots of times and once I think I even seen a sea monster with a—"

"No, Samuel. I'm afraid I've never heard of a book about a white whale. It can't be very popular."

His face fell.

"But this is a very interesting book. It's on etiquette."

"What's etiquette?"

"It's how to behave. You see, this book teaches you how to behave."

Samuel eyed the book suspiciously. "That don't sound interesting to me. You sure you don't got no books on white whales?"

"What have ya got there, Samuel my boy?" Mary asked.

"Supper," he announced, holding out the tray.

Mary got down off the bunk.

"What is it?" she asked, sniffing at it.

"Salted beef," he said, warily eyeing the gray, gristly lump. He looked up at us and shrugged. "I think."

"I know rotten horse when I see it," Mary scoffed.

Samuel nodded. "I wouldn't touch it. The first mate ate it and he's been puking up for hours now."

Mary snorted.

"And," Samuel said ominously, "the rats got to the breadstuffs."

"We are going to starve to death," Mary said in a firm voice.

"You say the first mate is ill?" I asked, curious.

Samuel nodded. "Jehu's puking up on deck right now. He looked green as an onion." The boy was quite fond of Jehu Scudder, the first mate, and followed him around like a puppy.

A wave smacked against the *Lady Luck,* and all at once the smell of the salted beef rose to my nose and the cabin seemed to close in on me. I swallowed hard.

"Ya look a bit green yourself, Jane my girl," Mary observed.

"Samuel," I said in an unsteady voice, "would you kindly escort me up on deck?"

"You ain't supposed to be up on deck, Miss Jane. Captain's orders," he said with a troubled look.

Captain Johnson had ordered Mary and me to remain below in the stuffy cabin but I often went above decks when I thought he would not be about. Captain Johnson was a furious Scot, always raging on about something. He hadn't permitted us to leave the ship when we put in at Valparaiso for fresh water or in

San Francisco for that matter. "If you leave this ship, you're not coming back on," he had informed us in his usual charming way.

To be plain, he hadn't even wanted to take us in the first place. "I don't abide women passengers. Women are nothing but bad luck," he'd said, spitting a huge wad of tobacco at my feet, a filthy habit if ever there was one. I didn't feel too bad as he'd told Father Joseph that priests were bad luck, too. It seemed to me that the only lucky creatures on the *Lady Luck* were the rats.

The ship rocked and I clutched my stomach.

I stood up shakily. "Take me on deck for some air or I shall be sick where I stand."

"All right, Miss Jane," Samuel said hastily. "You still don't got your sea legs? I never seen no one who ever took so long to get their legs," he said, shaking his head in amazement as he led me up on deck.

I clung to the rails, inhaling great big gulps of salty air, my stomach making an uneasy flip with each slap of a wave. It was mid-April. In Philadelphia the first colorful buds would be pushing up their heads, but here at sea, gray, gloomy skies marked the horizon. I pulled my cape tightly against the icy wind, remembering Miss Hepplewhite's Helpful Hints on Travel.

"Remember, Jane, a good traveler need only know three things. One, always keep your composure. Two, dress plainly and pack lightly. Three, do not let little irritations sway your cheery nature," Miss Hepplewhite had said, patting my shoulder.

She had been rather remiss in not mentioning any hints on killing fleas, avoiding rats, bathing with seawater, or being seasick.

"Obeying the captain again, I see," a voice said.

It was Jehu Scudder.

"Did you have the salted beef, too?" he asked ruefully.

I shook my head.

He nodded, rubbing self-consciously at the angry scar that slashed across his nose and right cheek. No doubt he had received it in a bar brawl like every other vulgar, ill-mannered sailor Papa had ever treated. Whoever had sewn it up had done a poor job. The scar was ragged, with raw-looking pink edges that stood out brightly on his tanned face. Papa would say that the fishmonger could have done better.

The ship rolled hard, and my stomach grumbled in a most disturbing way. I breathed deeply, willing it to calm.

"Still haven't got the legs?" Jehu observed.

I shook my head violently and leaned over the ship to be sick, but then the feeling passed. Getting one's sea legs apparently meant adjusting to the rocking of the ship. I rather doubted I would ever, as these men said, get my legs. All I seemed to get was seasick.

"It's better if you puke on the leeward side of the ship," Jehu said, pointing. "Then it won't blow back in your face."

"Oh blast you, Mr. Scudder," I said, clutching my heaving belly, cursing myself for cursing. Miss Hepplewhite always said that young ladies should never use foul language. "Loose tongues mean loose morals, girls," Miss Hepplewhite preached.

Jehu seemed unfazed by my words. "So tell me, Miss Peck. Why are you making this trip?"

Even though I had been on the *Lady Luck* for many months, I had not circulated much with the crew and hardly knew what to say.

There were twenty-five men, but only three of them were American—Jehu Scudder, Samuel, and Sturgis the surgeon. The rest were foreigners—Scandinavians, English, Spaniards, Irishmen, and Italians. Most of them had shown up inebriated at the docks, having drunk their wages the night before our departure. No liquor was allowed on board except for medicinal purposes, which seemed to me a very sensible precaution.

I hesitated. Deportment on the Street (Chapter Thirteen) discouraged conversation with gentlemen when not accompanied by a chaperone. I also imagined it discouraged conversation when one was seasick.

"My betrothed is on Shoalwater Bay," I said at last.

"Your betrothed," he said, studying me. "Long way to go to get married, especially a young lady like you. What's he doing there?"

"He is endeavoring to start a timber business."

Jehu looked at me with sharp eyes. "Hard work, that."

"William is very capable. He's a surgeon."

"You're marrying a bloody sawbones, you say?" he said, looking out to sea, not sounding the least bit impressed. He looked over at me, rubbing his scar. "I never met a sawbones worth a bean."

The man was rude.

"I'll have you know, my father is also a surgeon. And furthermore, William will be a wonderful husband. He's already built us a splendid house. Two stories with windows and an iron stove," I said, feeling unaccountably defensive. Oh dear, why had I told a falsehood? In actual fact William had been rather vague on the subject of where we were setting up house, and had written only that he'd arranged comfortable accommodations for us.

"A stove, you say," Jehu said dryly, eyes twinkling. "You're gonna need it to stay warm."

Jehu was most disconcertingly forward. "Mr. Scudder—"

But at that moment, the ship pitched wildly and I tumbled into him. A wave of nausea washed over me and then passed.

As the ship gained equilibrium, Jehu held me firmly, steadying my footing. His chest felt warm against my back, I realized with dawning horror. Miss Hepplewhite always said that a young lady should never allow a man to touch any part of her body, not even her elbow, and here was Jehu Scudder holding *all of me*!

"I beg your pardon, Mr. Scudder," I said, attempting to extricate myself.

Then my stomach heaved and I was sick all over his boots. When I looked up, he looked a bit ill himself.

"The pleasure was all mine," he said.

CHAPTER FIVE
or,
A Cheerful Countenance

"A true lady is ever cheerful," Miss Hepplewhite liked to say.

But I was having a hard time being cheerful in the face of Mary's fevered moaning. I was terribly worried.

Several days had passed, and the rat bite on her arm was now oozing a putrid yellow pus. Angry red welts streaked up to her neck. I remembered a patient of my father's, an orphan child, who'd been bitten by a rat and later died. "The damnable creatures make disgusting wounds, Janey," Papa had sighed at the time. Just thinking of him made me wish he were here, although our parting had been strained. He had given his permission, but never his blessing.

I summoned the ship's surgeon.

"I could lop off the arm," Sturgis offered. He belched loudly, and the cabin was suddenly redolent with the smell of whiskey. It was rumored that he drank the liquor intended for his patients.

I shuddered.

"Well? Do you want me to lop it off?" Sturgis barked. I looked at his bloodshot eyes and wondered at the wisdom of letting the man near Mary. He wasn't any class of surgeon that I could tell. One thing was certain. I was determined that Mary would not lose her arm.

"No," I said.

"There's always puking."

Many physicians believed that having a patient puke removed the bad poisons from the body. But as we had spent most of the voyage puking, I hardly saw the value in this remedy.

"I can honestly say that puking has done nothing to improve her health thus far."

"Then I reckon we could bleed her," he said, rubbing a hand through his greasy hair. Little white flecks fell to his shoulders.

I remembered Papa's feelings on bloodletting.

Sturgis picked up a knife and bared Mary's pale arm. The blue vein beneath her skin seemed so frail.

"No bleeding," I said firmly. "We can lance the wound." I hesitated, casting a suspicious eye at his dirt-encrusted fingernails. "I shall do it."

Sturgis belched again. "You?"

"Yes," I said, pulling myself up. "My father's a surgeon."

He shrugged and stepped aside. I took one of Sturgis's knives. I was thankful that Mary was in a swoon.

"Know what you're about there, girl?" Sturgis asked skeptically.

"Yes, of course," I said quickly.

It wasn't exactly the truth, although I had learned quite a bit from watching my father before I'd entered Miss Hepplewhite's school. I had seen Papa lance any number of boils. It was not unlike carving into a rotten apple that had been left too long in the sun.

I sliced gently into the inflamed wound, and the smell of rotting flesh filled the cabin. Believe me when I say that I very much wanted to rush outside and get sick, but I imagined Papa standing there with a rueful grin on his face.

"It's dirty work helping sick people," he would say. "But it's even dirtier work burying them."

I swallowed hard and steadied my resolve. I used my best needle and a piece of silk thread to stitch it up. Mary's face was waxy, and she didn't stir.

"There," I said, meeting Sturgis's bloodshot eyes.

"Not bad, girl. You're good with the needle."

I looked at Mary's arm. The stitches were straight, small, and neat. I could almost see Papa's proud smile. "Well done, Janey," he would have said. "Well done."

"Thank you," I said with a shaky smile. "I had a good teacher."

Father Joseph agreed to watch Mary while I went above to get some air. I was exhausted from taking care of her, and worse, I was frightened. What if she didn't recover? It would be all my fault.

The sky was just beginning to turn a dusky pink, the salty air bracing. I looked out at the ocean, at the endless rolling waves, and wondered wildly if we would ever reach Shoalwater Bay.

Would we ever be off this ship? My childhood dreams of sailing seemed very silly now.

The only thing that made this long, dreadful trip bearable was the knowledge that William was waiting for me at the other end of it. I clung to this thought even as I clung to the rail.

Captain Johnson was stomping about, shouting out orders. He caught sight of me and roared, "What are ya doing up here, lassie?"

I shook my head wordlessly. The captain scared me fairly to death.

"Well?" he hollered.

"I'll take responsibility for her, sir," a voice behind me said.

It was Jehu Scudder. He met the captain's gaze with steady eyes.

The captain grimaced and then wandered off, no doubt to shout at some other poor soul.

"Thank you," I said in a low voice.

Jehu nodded.

"Heard from Sturgis that Mary's taken a bad turn," he said. "Think she'll make it?"

It seemed somehow worse hearing him give voice to my worry. I thought of Miss Hepplewhite's advice to always be cheerful.

"I'm sure she'll get better," I said, forcing myself to smile.

He looked at me carefully, as if he didn't quite believe me, and then nodded shortly and stared out at the water.

I suddenly felt nervous to be standing here, unescorted, with this strange man. I struggled to remember Miss Hepplewhite's advice on such situations. Rules of Conversation (Chapter Two) had much to say about how to properly request the salt or discuss the latest play, but I didn't recall it mentioning how to converse with a sailor.

"Have you been to Shoalwater Bay before?" I asked finally.

He shook his head. "No. First time for the captain and me. We'll be taking on timber."

It was just my luck that I was on a ship with a captain who had never been where we were going.

"We are not lost, are we?" I asked suspiciously.

"Have no fear, we're on course by the wind."

This was hardly consoling. I had many fears, and now chief among them was the captain's ability to get us to our destination in one piece.

"Will we ever arrive?" I asked, exasperated.

He looked genuinely surprised. "We're making good time. The *Lady*'s a fast girl, one of the fastest brigs to come out of Philadelphia in a while. In fact, Samuel and I have a bet."

"A bet?"

"The number of days it will take us to get from Philadelphia to Shoalwater Bay."

"What is Samuel's opinion?"

Jehu surveyed the cloudless sky, tilting his scarred cheek to catch the ocean breeze. "Samuel thinks she's a lucky ship and that we'll make it in one hundred and eighty days, including our stops."

"And you?"

He grinned. "I believe in luck myself, but I also believe in spring squalls. I reckon we'll sight Shoalwater Bay in one hundred and ninety days."

If Samuel were right, that meant we were less than a week away. It couldn't be soon enough for me.

I looked out at the waves. "My father has this foolish saying. He says you make your own luck."

"He's right."

I thought of Sally Biddle and that rotten apple. "Well, I don't agree. I've been plagued by bad luck since I was eleven."

He looked at me steadily. "Maybe it's time you did something about that."

I retired below to check on Mary and relieve Father Joseph of his duties. She was awake.

"Are you feeling better, Mary?" I asked, pushing the hair off her forehead. Her head was cool, I was pleased to see. The fever was gone.

Mary smiled faintly through chapped lips. "Well enough, considering ya've been practicing yer stitchery on my arm, Jane my girl."

"You should be thankful I didn't embroider a violet on it," I teased.

She giggled, and I felt immediately better. She would be fine after all. Perhaps we would finally both get a decent night's rest for a change, I thought as I tugged my woolen nightdress over my head.

The door banged open, startling us both. I snatched up a

shawl. I imagined it was probably Father Joseph returning to give us another sermon about the savages. But it was not.

Jehu Scudder stood in the doorway, holding a tureen.

"I brought something for Mary," he said shortly, stepping inside. He was so tall and broad that he had to crouch to get into the small cabin.

Mary was in her bunk, covers up to her chin, but I was in plain sight, wearing only a woolen nightdress and a shawl. Most shockingly, my stocking-covered ankles were clearly visible! Quickly I tucked my feet beneath the hem of the nightdress, lest Jehu see them.

The words rose in my throat to tell him to leave, that it wasn't at all proper for him to be in our cabin when we weren't properly dressed, but before I could say anything he pulled up a chair as if he meant to stay.

"Here," he said, passing me the tureen.

I sniffed at the broth to make certain it wasn't bilge water, but it smelled deliciously of chicken.

"It's a miracle the cook made something decent," I said.

"Cook didn't make it. I did."

"You did?" I was shocked.

He tilted his head in acknowledgment. In the shadowy light of the lantern his scar seemed less visible, and I suddenly realized that he had bright, blue eyes. Strange, that I had never noticed his eyes before.

"And there's no horse meat in there, I promise," he added, smiling. He looked less fearsome when he smiled.

I spooned the broth into Mary's mouth while she observed us through slit eyes. The cabin was as silent as our parlor when I was a young girl and practicing listening well. Miss Hepplewhite always said that it was a lady's obligation to encourage good conversation when in polite company, but I was having a difficult time considering Jehu polite company, for all that he had brought the broth. Moreover, I could not help feeling conscious of my ankles. Even William had never seen my stocking-covered ankles!

At last I spoke. "Where did you learn to cook?"

He shrugged. "On ships, I suppose. Been at sea since I was Samuel's age. If you want something good to eat, you best make it yourself. First lesson I learned."

"Oh."

He looked at me. "And you? Are you a good cook?"

I hesitated, and then shook my head. "We always had Mrs. Parker."

He nodded. Was that a flicker of disappointment in his eyes?

"And of course Mary is a very fine cook," I said quickly. "She is planning to open a boardinghouse and make her fortune when we reach the frontier. Aren't you, Mary?"

Mary made a small sound.

"So, Miss Peck, how will you spend your days on the frontier if you won't be cooking?" he asked.

I bit my lip, momentarily perplexed. "I suppose I'll embroider."

"Embroider, eh?" He looked at Mary dubiously.

"Yes, embroider," I said firmly.

"There's a big demand for needlepoint cushions on the

frontier, then, is there?" Now there was a flicker of something else in his eyes. Amusement?

From her bunk Mary chuckled quietly. She was most certainly feeling better.

Jehu took a deep breath and stood up. "Well, Miss Peck, if you want my advice, you might want to ask Mary here for some tips on cooking and the like."

I shrugged as if unconcerned. "I'm sure William has already employed a maid and a cook for us."

Jehu squinted at the two of us. "For your sake, I hope so."

Although Mary was better, she was still weak. Not long after Jehu left, she was snoring lightly, so I took the opportunity to undo my braid and give my hair a good brushing. I was working on a particularly frustrating snarl when Jehu banged on the door and barged into our cabin for the second time that evening.

Jehu stared at my hair tumbling loose around my shoulders, a strange expression on his face. It was most improper for a man to see a young lady with her hair unbound, almost as bad as seeing her bare ankles.

"Do you never knock?" I demanded.

"You should try rum."

"I beg your pardon?"

"New England rum. It's good for the tangles."

I felt myself go red. "Was there something you required?" I asked stiffly.

Jehu remembered himself. "We're sailing straight into a storm. Batten down everything and stay below decks." And then he disappeared as quickly as he had come.

In short order the ship began rocking wildly, and we were soon joined by Father Joseph and Sturgis. It seemed that their cabin was taking in water.

The wind rose to a keening howl, and the *Lady Luck* began careening with frightful violence, side to side and up and down. The screeching wind drowned out the shouts of the sailors above deck. The lantern swung wildly as the ship tilted to and fro, casting fearful shadows in the small cabin.

Mary was pale as a wraith, and Father Joseph's eyebrows twitched madly as he clutched the table with real terror. Only Sturgis was unaffected by the rough seas, no doubt because of all the whiskey in his belly.

"This is a witch of a storm all right," Sturgis slurred, slumped in a corner, nursing his bottle.

"Jane my girl," Mary croaked weakly. "Do ya think we'll make it to this blessed Shoalwater Bay?"

A true lady is ever cheerful.

"Yes, of course," I said brightly, although fear was racing up and down my spine.

Then, without warning, something smashed into the ship with such force that I went tumbling from my chair onto the floor. It felt like a whale or some huge sea monster had struck us. I struggled to right my chair against the rocking of the ship.

Even Sturgis paled. "That didn't sound good."

"Sweet Dieu, have mercy on your children," Father Joseph whispered, patting his forehead nervously.

The door to the cabin flew open, and Jehu's slick face appeared. He was soaking wet.

"Come on, man!" he shouted to Sturgis. "Samuel's been hurt!" And then he was gone.

Samuel? I thought in horror.

"Jane my girl," Mary said hoarsely. She was thinking the same thing I was. Sturgis was too drunk to be of help to anyone, let alone sweet Samuel.

Sturgis lurched drunkenly to his feet. I pushed him back down.

"What are you about, girl?" he demanded belligerently.

"Stay with Mary," I said firmly, and was out the door before he could argue.

Shall I ever forget the sight that met my eyes? The screaming men, the pelting rain, the way the angry black waves seemed to reach from the very depths of the sea like giant hands trying to drag the ship down. A flash of lightning struck the ocean, illuminating the deck for one long, terrible moment, and I saw at once the cause of the horrible sound. The mainmast had been struck by lightning, and the topsail yard had crashed down to the deck in a tangle of rigging, sailcloth, and splintered wood. The heaviest chunk had landed horribly on Samuel. Deckhands were swarming about, brandishing knives, trying to free the boy.

The ship tipped, and I went tumbling to the deck. I pushed

myself to my feet and rushed over fallen debris to Samuel, grabbing his hand.

"Oh blast," I whispered, taking in the sight, my heart lurching sickly.

A piece of wood was stretched across the boy's belly, pinning him down, and blood gushed down his head. So much blood! He looked up at me with blank eyes.

"Mama?" he said. There was a dazed expression on his face.

Someone was shaking my shoulders.

"Where's the blasted sawbones?" Jehu shouted, his face slick with rain.

"He's drunk!"

"Don't you have any sense? It's dangerous up here! Get below now!" Jehu shouted in a frustrated voice, the scar on his cheek twitching.

"I can't just leave him!"

"It's an order!"

Miss Hepplewhite said a young lady was obedient in all things, but all I could hear was Papa saying, "A doctor never abandons a patient in need, Janey."

"I'm staying!" I yelled.

Jehu's lips thinned into a harsh line, and he nodded shortly. He turned and shouted to two men to come take hold of the yard.

Samuel clutched my hand.

"Mama?" he asked anxiously. I sank to my knees and put his head in my lap, brushing the hair from his face.

"Yes, Samuel, it's Mama," I said, trying to sound cheery.

The blood from his head was a spreading bloom on my skirt. "Everything's going to be just fine."

My presence calmed him, and he settled in my arms.

"Heave now!" Jehu shouted, his face to the wind.

And as the yard lifted, the boy jerked awake for a moment, his eyes bright with pain. Then he sighed and closed his eyes, resting his head on my lap as gently as if he were falling asleep, his eyelashes dark, wet spikes on his soft, young cheeks.

"Samuel!" I cried, but he didn't stir.

Jehu looked at me with dark, unfathomable eyes.

"I'm sorry, Jane."

I struggled back to the cabin, hair plastered to my face, soaking wet and shaking.

The first thing I saw was Father Joseph's black-robed back. He was kneeling next to Mary's bunk, praying.

"What are you doing?" I whispered.

Sturgis roused himself. "The girl fell from the bunk when we tipped and struck her head. I couldn't do anything for her."

"What?" The word tumbled from my mouth, spoken by some other girl, not me, not Jane Peck.

"She is dead, mademoiselle," Father Joseph said, shaking his head sadly at me.

"No," I whispered, wiping my hand across my face as if to wipe away the sight. "She can't be. I was only gone for a moment."

"I'm sorry, mademoiselle," Father Joseph said, an eerie echo of Jehu's words.

I looked over at the bunk, at Mary's white face, at the blood matting her thick, black hair, at her dark eyes staring sightlessly at the ceiling, and all I could do was stand there. The wind and the rain sprayed through the open door, and the lantern shook crazily. It seemed easier just to *be*, to let the storm beat upon me, scream at my back, howl in my ear.

"We must pray for her sins," Father Joseph urged.

The priest leaned forward to touch Mary's forehead, and the sight of him touching her white skin shook something inside me, something so deep that it stabbed my very soul, and I screamed.

"No!"

I screamed and screamed, my voice rising with the wind, flying out the door, disappearing into the dark night as if the word alone could bring her back, bring back her merry eyes, her laughing mouth, her warm heart. Bring back Mary Hearn. A sweet girl. A good cook. A lively companion. The finest brusher of horrible, ratty, tangled red hair in all of Philadelphia.

My only true friend in the whole world.

Tears ran down my cheeks as Jehu Scudder came running into the cabin, knife drawn.

"What is it?" Jehu demanded.

"The girl's dead," Sturgis shouted over the wind. "Ain't my fault."

A cold fury rushed through me. I couldn't stand the sight of him.

"I left her with you!" I howled. "Why didn't you keep her from falling? Why couldn't you do something useful for a change instead of drink?"

I flung myself at Sturgis, hair flying. I wanted to kill that careless, heartless man, I wanted to rip his eyes out with my own two hands, but I was weeping so hard that I could barely see, and Sturgis was stumbling back in surprise and Father Joseph was shouting at me, and the next thing I knew someone grabbed me around the waist and hauled me back.

"Jane!" Jehu said grimly, his arm tight around my middle. "There's nothing you can do."

The fury went out of me in a rush, leaving me limp with grief.

"If I had just stayed," I cried brokenly, weeping into his chest. "If I had just stayed!"

Jehu said nothing, just rubbed his hand down my back soothingly, his fingers tangling in my hair like Mary's brush.

We stood there in the doorway and I wept and wept while the wind and the rain pounded in through the dark, terrible night.

I sewed the burial shrouds out of sheets meant for my marriage bed. My stitches were straight and perfect. Miss Hepplewhite would have been proud.

We buried young Samuel and Mary at sea, beneath the same blue wave.

CHAPTER SIX
or,
The Importance of Punctuality

White loamy breakers and the raucous cry of seagulls signaled land.

The men's laughter sang out across the water as the *Lady Luck* limped into a bright, sparkling bay, the water glassy as a mirror. I stood on the deck and let the warm April breeze tangle my hair.

I had spent the rest of the voyage numb, too numb even to be seasick. Mary's empty bunk haunted me. I kept thinking I would wake and hear her merry voice, but the only sound I heard was the endless slap of waves against the ship.

And now, at last, we were in Shoalwater Bay.

My breath caught at the astonishing sight. I, who had grown up with cobblestone streets and brick buildings, was now surrounded on every side by wild green wilderness. Never in my entire life had I seen anything so raw and vast. Sunlight skipped across the shimmering water, and sleek creatures slipped between the waves like playful puppies. I leaned over to get a better look at the strange animals.

"They're sea otters," Jehu said in a soft voice, coming to stand next to me.

I nodded.

Jehu stared into the distance. "Seems Samuel was right after all." He whispered, "One hundred and eighty days exactly."

His roughened hands gripped the rail, and the sight of those white knuckles reminded me of that terrible night at sea. For a moment Mary's white face rose before me, but I pushed her away, pushed her down deep to a place where I could forget.

Jehu shook his head as if to push away his own thoughts and looked at me.

"You sure have a lot of green dresses," he said.

"William says I look beautiful in green," I said defensively.

"He does, does he?" Jehu said, a sarcastic edge to his voice. He sounded just like Papa.

I stared stubbornly out at the waves. I couldn't wait to be off this ship and away from this man. I couldn't wait to see William. William with his beautiful eyes and lovely manners.

Jehu studied me with hooded eyes. "I think blue would suit you better."

Before I could retort that a grubby sailor was perhaps the last person on earth who should be giving hints on fashion, the men started shouting. I craned my neck to see what the excitement was about.

Paddling right toward the *Lady Luck* was a long canoe—full of savages!

The canoe was sleek as a bird, cutting through the water as

cleanly as a knife through pie. A stout white man sporting a shaggy white mustache and beard sat in the middle of the canoe and waved madly.

"Ho there!" the man called as the canoe pulled alongside the *Lady Luck,* bobbing in the waves. "Capital day, is it not?"

I couldn't take my eyes off the savages. Their complexions were coppery and they had broad noses. But strangest of all, the front of their foreheads appeared, well, flattened. They seemed to regard me with such ferocious expressions that I backed away from the rail.

"Your name, sir," Father Joseph called down imperiously.

The white man's face filled with mirth and he shouted back, "James G. Swan, at your service, Father!"

"And I am Father Joseph Lionnet, lately of Montreal."

The jolly Mr. Swan turned his attention on me and beamed. "And you, young lady, must be Miss Peck," he declared.

I was astonished. How did this strange man know my name?

"I am, sir. How did you know?"

"Young William told me all about you and your lovely red hair. His description did not do you justice, I'm afraid," Mr. Swan said with a jolly smile.

William! I thought with a rush of excitement. He had spoken of me!

"Welcome, Jane Peck," Mr. Swan boomed, "to Shoalwater Bay."

The canoe accompanied us to the shore, where the *Lady Luck* dropped anchor and a small rowboat was lowered.

I peered nervously over the side of the ship. The climb from the deck to the rowboat waiting below was very high. Father Joseph, Captain Johnson, Jehu, and the other men going ashore were already in the rowboat, waiting for me.

"C'mon, lassie," Captain Johnson barked. "We're not waiting all day."

I straightened my bonnet and set one foot tentatively onto the rope ladder, holding on to the rungs. Think of William, I told myself bravely.

The ladder started to swing wildly before I even got my other foot down.

My bonnet promptly slipped forward in front of my eyes.

"Blast," I whispered as I clung to the ladder for dear life, trying to decide how to muddle my way out.

I pushed the bonnet back.

"You all right up there?" Jehu called.

"I am very well, thank you," I replied tersely. Or I would be as soon as the rope ladder stopped swinging and my belly calmed.

I took a deep breath and steadied myself, starting slowly down the next rung, and then the next, concentrating only on the rungs in front of me. It was almost easy if I pretended I was descending a carriage the way Miss Hepplewhite had demonstrated. Except, of course, I was doing it backward and suspended over water! I was almost all the way down when I felt a sudden rush of air on my legs and one of the men in the rowboat below whistled wolfishly.

My skirt had snagged on a rung and my stockinged legs were exposed for all the world to see! I blushed as red as my hair.

"Trying to make a good impression with the locals, eh Jane?" Jehu chuckled. Truly he was the most disagreeable man I'd ever laid eyes on.

"That's Miss Peck to you," I said in a cool voice.

Jehu narrowed his eyes. "Of course, Miss Peck," he said, handing me down into the boat.

I settled onto a bench, and a filthy sailor with a rotten front tooth leered at me. I looked quickly away.

We bounced up and down on the waves as the men rowed to shore. I scanned the group awaiting us on the dark sand. Not one of them had William's bright blond hair. Was he not there? Where was he?

It was an altogether strange greeting party, and I eyed them with trepidation. Upon closer inspection the savages were dressed like white men and not like the illustrations in the newspapers. Their hair was thick and black, and most wore it long and parted down the middle.

Captain Johnson leaped off the boat and strode through the shallow water to the beach. Jehu put out a hand. I regarded him warily.

He sighed, "Come on, Miss Peck. I'll not bite, but I can't speak for the men on shore."

I reluctantly extended my gloved hand. Imagine my surprise and astonishment when he ignored it—and swung me up into his arms!

"Kindly put me down," I said stiffly.

He waded through the water, ignoring me. "Can't be getting

your skirts wet when you're meeting your betrothed, now can you?"

When we reached the shore, he set me down. Need I say I was heartily glad to be on solid ground after so many months at sea? Even so, the ground seemed to move as if we were still on the ship. I clutched Jehu's arm for a moment as a wave of nausea washed over me.

"All right?" he asked. "Sometimes when you've been seasick it takes time to get your land legs back."

I nodded, swallowing hard, praying that I would not be sick in front of all these men, who were busy making introductions.

"Johnson," Captain Johnson said brusquely. "Captain of the *Lady Luck*."

"I am James Swan, Captain," the stocky, plump-bellied man declared with a wide smile. Mr. Swan's ill-fitting wire-rimmed spectacles were patched with twine and balanced precariously on his bulbous nose. "How long was your voyage, my good man?"

"One hundred and eighty days from Philadelphia," Captain Johnson said with a slow grin.

"Capital time, my dear fellow! Capital! And what brings you to our fair country?"

"Timber."

"Capital! A man after my own heart." Mr. Swan turned to the scruffy-looking mountain man next to him. "This is Mr. Russell, longtime resident of Shoalwater Bay."

The man, with a mangy, gray-flecked beard, was outfitted entirely in buckskins, a rifle slung over his back.

"Mr. Russell runs our humble trading post, such as it is," Mr. Swan explained.

Mr. Russell narrowed his eyes at me, spat on the ground, and snorted. Whoever he was, he was plainly not a very pleasant man.

An older man stepped forward.

"And this is Toke. He is the *tyee*, chief, of the Chinooks of Shoalwater Bay," Mr. Swan said with a flourish.

I must admit, I was rather surprised. I had imagined someone younger and fiercer, with a long, sharp nose, war paint, and a necklace of human teeth. Instead, as he fixed me with his appraising, intelligent gaze, I was rather reminded of the dignified judge Papa invited over for supper. Except the judge had been better dressed. All that kept us from seeing Chief Toke in his natural state was the belt holding the blanket wrapped around him.

A leathery-looking thing hung from the side of his belt. I recalled stories from newspapers and shivered, although the chief looked perfectly harmless, and perhaps even kind.

"Is that a scalp?" I whispered to Mr. Swan.

Mr. Swan blinked. "A scalp?"

"Yes, a scalp. From some unfortunate pioneer."

"It's the sole of an old shoe," Mr. Russell grunted.

"I beg your pardon?"

Chief Toke fingered the leather.

"A shoe. He likes to carry it around. Used to be mine." Mr. Russell spit a wad of tobacco, and it barely missed my toe. It seemed that the loathsome habits of the States had been carried to the frontier.

"I see," I said, although I clearly did not.

"Mr. Russell is a great friend of Toke's people," Mr. Swan said as if this explained everything.

"Right," Captain Johnson said. "Well. This here is my first mate, Jehu Scudder. This is Father Joseph, and the girl is Jane Peck."

"It is a pleasure to meet you, Mr. Scudder, Father," Mr. Swan said, shaking the men's hands firmly. He smiled when he reached me. "It is indeed a surprise to see you, Miss Peck, although I daresay I feel as if I already know you. William spoke often about you!"

"A surprise to see me?" I asked. And where was William?

But Mr. Swan had already turned away and was deep in conversation with the chief.

"*King George tillicum*," Mr. Swan said, pointing to Captain Johnson. Chief Toke nodded gravely. "*Boston tillicum*." Mr. Swan gestured to me. "Jane Peck."

"You speak the savage's language?" Father Joseph asked in an amazed voice.

"I speak the Jargon. Most of the folks around here do."

"The Jargon?"

"It's a kind of trading language. Mainly Chinook and some English and French all mixed together. It's not elegant, but we get by."

"What did you tell him?" Father Joseph asked.

"I told him that Captain Johnson was English and that Miss Peck was an American," Mr. Swan said.

"But you pointed to me and said Boston. I'm not from Boston; I'm from Philadelphia," I said.

"The first ships that came from the States were from Boston, so now the Indians call all Americans *Boston tillicum*, Boston people. They call the British *King George tillicum*, on account of King George."

"Mr. Swan, what did you mean when you said you were surprised to see me? Where is William?" I asked, my voice rising a notch.

"Well, I believe you were supposed to have arrived over two months ago." He paused. "And I'm afraid William's not here."

"Not here?" I whispered, my heart and belly twisting painfully.

Mr. Swan frowned. "William was called away on an errand for the governor."

William wasn't here!

"As an Indian agent, your future husband is much in demand, I'm afraid. He left for parts north several weeks ago."

It was too much. I rushed over to the water and retched up my breakfast. This wasn't happening, I told myself, trying to catch my breath. I remembered every word Papa had said about William. How he was a fool and had no sense. I touched my hand to my belly, trying to compose myself.

"You okay?"

Jehu put a hand on my arm. I shook it off angrily and marched back to where the men were all standing, staring at me as if I had two heads.

"Are you all right, my dear?" Mr. Swan asked.

"Didn't William receive my letter saying that our departure had been delayed?" I asked, shaking and pale.

"I'm afraid not, my dear." He shrugged good-naturedly. "The

mail is not very reliable out here. When you didn't arrive two months ago as you'd written when you accepted his proposal, William thought you'd changed your mind and thought it best to go about his business."

"Changed my mind? How could he think such a thing? I didn't!" I said desperately. "It took two months to get my wedding dress made so we were late leaving and, and—"

Mr. Swan shook his head sadly at me.

Miss Hepplewhite's words rang in my ears:

Young ladies who are not punctual when traveling think up any manner of excuses. The truth is the unpunctual do not allow themselves sufficient time.

I burst into tears.

"There, there," Mr. Swan said comfortingly, handing me a square of rough cloth. "There's nothing to cry about. He'll turn up eventually."

I looked up at him through tears and sniffed. "But when?"

Mr. Swan looked perplexed. "I'm sorry, dear girl, but I can't say for certain."

"Can't we send word for him to come back?"

"It's not that simple out here, my dear Miss Peck. It's best to just wait for his return."

"What exactly am I supposed to do until then?" I asked. The difficulty of my situation was just beginning to occur to me. "Who will look after me?"

"I'm sure we'll sort everything out." Mr. Swan clapped his hands efficiently. "I suggest we get you and your companions acquainted with the surroundings," he said, pushing up his spectacles. He turned and started purposefully down the trail, the men following him into the deep, dark woods.

All I could do was stand there and watch them go, too stunned to move.

Jehu leaned over and said gently, "Come on, Jane."

What was I going to do? I thought wildly as I followed the men through the dense forest. What would happen to me?

This wilderness bore no resemblance to the familiar woods of Pennsylvania. The very trees were different—so massive that they reached the sky. The ferns grew huge and lush and spidery. Everywhere strange birds cried and fluttered.

"I have never seen trees this tall," Father Joseph said in awe.

"Yes, Father," Mr. Swan called back. "They are peculiar to this region. They are most wondrous, are they not?"

"Wondrous to chop down," Captain Johnson said, a gleam in his eye.

The trail emptied into a wide clearing, at the center of which a solitary, shabby-looking log cabin was situated. A group of savages congregated in front of it.

I froze when I caught sight of the women. I couldn't believe my eyes.

Most of the women were wearing ordinary dresses of calico, but a few were wearing scandalous-looking skirts that ended above the knee. Bare knees, legs, and ankles were in *plain* sight! Furthermore, none of the women were wearing shoes!

The women stared at me boldly.

I hung back, afraid and nervous.

"Here we are," Mr. Swan said in a satisfied voice.

"Is this where the savages live?" I asked.

Mr. Swan looked confused. "No, this is Mr. Russell's cabin, and our humble home. It doubles as our trading post as well. Toke's lodge is a stone's throw away, just down that stream." He pointed to a stream that ran alongside the encampment.

But I couldn't take my eyes from the strange sight in front of me. One of the savage women had tied a baby's head between a board and a sort of padded cradle and secured it with a length of fabric, squeezing the infant's forehead! No doubt this was how they acquired their flattened foreheads.

I tugged on Mr. Swan's hand.

"Yes, my dear?"

"Mr. Swan," I whispered, "she's torturing that infant!"

The infant in question was fast asleep.

Mr. Swan winked. "The babe looks well enough to me."

He started toward the cabin.

I looked about me, but there were no other lodgings to be seen. Perhaps William's house was farther down the path, or in another area entirely.

"Mr. Swan," I called politely.

"Yes, Miss Peck?"

"Could you please direct me to William's house?"

Mr. Swan wrinkled his nose, and his spectacles slid a little lower down his face. "William's house?"

"Yes."

"Well. Hmmph. I'm rather afraid—" He cleared his throat. "I'm rather afraid William has no house of his own, my dear."

"What?" I asked, my voice wavering.

"He has always stayed with us in the cabin," he said simply.

I could hardly believe my ears. I was here on my own with nowhere to live? It was impossible. William would never do this to me. He was a gentleman. Certainly this was all a mistake!

"But surely there are other houses in the settlement?" I faltered.

Mr. Swan shifted uncomfortably. "Miss Peck. I'm afraid that the cabin *is* the settlement. I thought William had told you."

"Are there no houses at all?"

Mr. Russell narrowed his eyes at me and spat a wad of tobacco, narrowly missing my skirt. "Well, gal, I reckon ya've come to the wrong place if yar expecting bricks and steps."

"But William wrote that he'd arranged for 'comfortable accommodations,'" I said desperately, reciting William's words by heart.

Mr. Swan scratched his beard thoughtfully. "Well, Mr. Russell's cabin is very pleasant. Marvelously warm when the cold wind blows off the bay." He turned and started toward the cabin again.

I felt faint. William was missing. Mary was dead. Papa was far away. And here I was in the middle of the wilderness with no place to stay.

As I looked around anxiously, another realization struck home.

"Mr. Swan!" I called.

"Yes, Miss Peck?"

"Where are the other women?"

"Why, Miss Peck," Mr. Swan said, pushing his spectacles up. "They're right in front of you." He pointed to the group of savages.

"I meant the other *ladies*," I clarified.

"Oh," he said. "I'm afraid there aren't any others. You're the only one."

I swear I heard Sally Biddle laughing at me all the way back in Philadelphia.

CHAPTER SEVEN
or,
Being a Good Guest

I peered into the dark doorway of the miserable cabin. The floorboards of the porch creaked dangerously under my feet.

A motley gathering of filthy pioneer men and savages were sitting around on rough benches drinking whiskey. A rotten odor permeated the air. No doubt it came from the men themselves.

"Pardon me, but where am I to sleep?" I called from the doorway, holding my handkerchief to my nose. The men ignored me.

I knew that a gracious guest should not interfere with the domestic routine of the house, but the only routine here seemed to involve getting drunk. Clearly any instructions and helpful hints from Being a Good Guest (Chapter Eleven) would be wasted on this vulgar group.

I squinted through the single smoke-filled room. Two tiny windows covered with greasy-looking animal skins let in less light than the chinks in the walls. Hard-looking wooden bunks lined two walls. A rickety set of rough-hewn shelves burdened with sacks of flour, potatoes, and spices lined another wall. Every surface was covered with a thick layer of dust and grit. The floor was hard-packed dirt, and I could tell from the way the shadows moved that there was more than dirt on the floor. Vermin.

It was frightful.

Summoning all my courage, I walked into the room, and as I did something struck me in the face.

I looked up, startled.

An enormous dead cougar hung from the rafters, its teeth frozen in a snarl.

I screamed.

"What ya hollering for?" Mr. Russell drawled, his whiskers twitching.

"Where am I to sleep!" I shouted in sheer frustration.

A hush came over the room. All eyes fixed on me.

"Do any of you selfish louts understand what a lady requires?" I asked peevishly. Sometimes strong language is regrettable but necessary.

"Sleep?" Mr. Swan blinked and looked about. "Why, here, of course."

I was speechless.

"I'll be moving into my own home in a few weeks' time, and you will be most welcome there," Mr. Swan said kindly.

"Stay *here*?" I said at last. I was dumbfounded. Miss Hepplewhite didn't even consider it proper for unmarried ladies and gentlemen to sit on the same picnic blanket, and here was

Mr. Swan proposing that I *sleep* in the same room as these vulgar men! It was utterly unthinkable!

Mr. Swan gave me a fatherly smile and said reassuringly, "You have nothing to fear, Miss Peck."

I pulled myself up, smoothing my skirt and straightening my bonnet.

"Mr. Swan, I must protest. I can't possibly sleep here."

"We don't snore, gal," Mr. Russell said, spitting, and this time I swear he aimed right at my petticoats! I leaped back, barely avoiding the gob of wet, chewed tobacco. And to think that when I was a girl, I had considered spitting amusing.

"Well, Mr. Swan? There simply must be somewhere else I can stay," I said in a reasonable tone.

"I'm afraid, Miss Peck, there is nowhere else."

Before I could take in the enormity of Mr. Swan's words, a young savage about my age entered the doorway of the cabin carrying my trunk from the *Lady Luck.*

My mouth nearly dropped open in astonishment.

I had never seen such a handsome young man in all my life. Except William, of course, but even he seemed a hazy memory compared to this finely muscled body. The savage in question had liquid eyes, flowing hair, and a radiant smile, and despite myself, I stared at him. He was remarkably pleasing to the eye.

I stared at the comely young man and he grinned back at me, plainly amused and quite aware of his appeal. There was certainly something charming about him. I felt heat rise to my cheeks.

Jehu snorted.

"Miss Peck, may I introduce Handsome Jim?" Mr. Swan said formally.

Handsome Jim puffed out his chest and bowed. I swallowed and curtsied quickly.

"His name is truly Handsome Jim?" Father Joseph asked.

"I should say it suits him," I said before I could stop the words.

Mr. Swan laughed while I blushed at my indiscretion.

"I agree," Mr. Swan said, his eyes twinkling. "And he is most fond of our mirrors and admiring his reflection in the water. He used to be Handsome Tom, but he changed his name recently. Isn't that right, Jim?"

Handsome Jim looked suddenly nervous but nodded. It was clear enough that he understood English.

"Changed his name?" Father Joseph asked with a sniff of disdain. "These savages can't even remember their own names and must change them?"

Mr. Swan shook his head.

"My dear fellow, it is the habit of these Indians to change their names when one of their kin dies. It is their belief that the spirit of the departed soul comes back and haunts them, attempting to lure them to the other side. They change their names to fool the spirits."

Handsome Jim nodded sagely and said, "*Memelose tillicums.*"

"*Memelose tillicums* are dead people," Mr. Swan explained. "Spirits."

"How on earth do they keep track of each other if they change their names all the time?" I asked.

"With their eyes, gal," Mr. Russell said flatly.

"Where you want this?" Handsome Jim asked, gesturing to the trunk in the doorway.

"You may put my trunk there, for now," I said, turning my attention back to the matters at hand. "Mr. Swan, I can't possibly sleep here. You must see my position. It simply isn't proper."

Mr. Swan scratched his head and said finally, "I suppose we could fix you up a tent."

"A tent?" The cabin suddenly had its attractions. At least it had a roof.

Something small and furry scampered across the filthy dirt floor with a squeak, and I reconsidered.

"A tent will have to do until William returns," I said, resigned. I had never felt so utterly alone. I would have done anything to hear Papa's voice telling me that I was his favorite daughter.

Mr. Swan and Handsome Jim fitted up a small tent for me using a spare canvas sail. They flung the canvas over a sturdy-looking branch and secured it with wooden stakes. Handsome Jim gave me some mats woven from reeds to put on the ground. It seemed a very flimsy affair but would have to suffice for the time being.

"I've spent many a night under that sail. It's a good one," Mr. Swan said, surveying their work.

"I am in your debt, Mr. Swan."

"Miss Peck, are you certain that you really want to be sleeping out here?" They had set up the tent within plain sight of Mr. Russell's cabin. "It's much warmer in Mr. Russell's cabin, you know. There's plenty of room." Mr. Swan paused meaningfully. "And the spring rains can be very terrible. It is still April yet."

"I'll be perfectly fine. Thank you anyway," I declined politely.

"Thar's the varmints," Mr. Russell said. He had come outside, no doubt to spit at me.

What about the varmints in his cabin? I shook my head firmly. I preferred to take my chances outside.

Just then, a potbellied black dog raced up to us, took a flying leap in my direction, knocked me flat onto the ground, and set about licking my face enthusiastically.

Mr. Swan smiled. "Miss Peck, may I introduce Brandywine?"

I pushed the slobbering hound away.

"Blasted beast!"

My face was now sticky with dog drool and my dress covered with muddy paw prints and grass stains. All I could think was that I had to be clean that very instant.

"Mr. Swan," I asked, "could someone kindly draw me a warm bath?"

"Draw ya a bath?" Mr. Russell hooted.

"But surely one of the savages could—"

Mr. Swan interrupted me gently. "They are not servants, Miss Peck. And you ought not to call them savages. They are friends. And I'm sorry to say that we have no bathtub."

I stared at him. No bathtub? It was little wonder the men were so utterly filthy.

"But I'm sure the *Indian* women will be happy to conduct you to the spring to bathe. The Chinooks are great bathers, my dear. Much like the ancient Romans," Mr. Swan said. "I'll just go see."

I was rather surprised to hear that savage Indians bathed more often than white men, but upon closer inspection it appeared that they did. Mr. Russell looked downright greasy in his buckskins compared to Handsome Jim.

Mr. Swan went over to where the women were congregated and brought back an extremely pretty one with almond eyes and long, straight black hair tied back in a braid. She was wearing one of the scandalous skirts. A young girl trailed behind her.

"This is Suis. She is married to Chief Toke."

She seemed very young to be married to the older man, as she couldn't be more than twenty-five. Her eyes lingered on my hair.

"Is there no way to get some hot water for a bath?" I pleaded. "I haven't had a proper bath in months."

"Ain't news to me," Mr. Russell guffawed.

"You could greatly benefit from a bath yourself," I said stiffly, my patience exhausted. I turned to Mr. Swan, drawing myself up. "I can't go with them. It simply isn't safe. What if they try to scalp me?"

Mr. Swan chuckled. "They do seem to be rather taken with your red hair, don't they?"

I hastily tucked my hair under my bonnet and secured it tightly.

"Miss Peck," Mr. Swan laughed, his belly rolling. "The Chinooks do not scalp. At least these don't. You'll be quite safe."

"But they're savage Indians!" I said, my voice rising.

He peered at me through his spectacles. "Not savages, my dear, but Indians, certainly."

"You make no sense!" I cried wildly. "How can they be safe?"

Mr. Swan winked. "When in Indian country, it is always safest to travel with Indians."

I clutched a passably clean towel and the last bar of lavender soap from my trunk and viewed the two women with trepidation. We stood there for a moment, studying each other. Suis looked very much as if she wanted to yank my hair.

"I am Miss Jane Peck," I said with a slight curtsy, wondering why I even bothered. I entertained little hope of proper conversation from such ignorant creatures. They didn't even have enough sense not to go around half-naked.

"I am Suis. Come," the woman said, to my astonishment.

"You speak English?" I asked.

She nodded simply. "I speak English, Chinook, and Jargon."

Suis started down a narrow path into the dark, thick woods, and the younger girl followed her. Her head was round, not slanted like Suis's, and her ankles were swollen like those of the girls who worked in the factories in Philadelphia.

I tried to keep up with Suis, but my shoes sank in the muddy trail, and I tripped on my petticoats no matter how high I held them. Miss Hepplewhite would have been very upset to see such draggled petticoats.

Suis stopped abruptly in front of a sparkling clear spring that looked altogether inviting after the long months at sea. The young girl joined her, and the two of them sat down on a log. For a long moment I stood there, clutching my soap and towel. Was I really to bathe under their watchful eyes? The only people who had ever seen me naked were Mary and Mrs. Parker.

"Thank you," I said with a tight smile. "You can go back now. I'll be fine. Really."

But Suis and the girl just sat there and stared at me. Clearly they had no intention of leaving.

Seeing that I had little option if I wanted a bath, I went behind a thick bush and took off my muddy dress and petticoats. I decided it was best to leave on my corset and pantaloons, for modesty's sake. I also left on my bonnet as a precaution.

When I reappeared from behind the bush Suis's eyes went wide. She removed one of the elaborate shell necklaces adorning her neck and held it out in offering.

"You want trade?" she asked, pointing at my corset.

"You want my corset?"

"I trade *hiqua* for colset," she said, saying the new word almost perfectly except for the *r*.

I hesitated.

"Trade?" Suis demanded.

I did not want to give offense. She was married to the chief, after all. But I needed the corset. It was the only one I had packed. "A respectable young lady never goes out without a corset," Miss Hepplewhite had advised. It was no trifling matter to give it up. Still I couldn't help but hear Papa's voice. "There is nothing fashionable about crushed organs, Janey," he had said.

"Trade?" Suis repeated.

"No, thank you," I said in a polite but firm voice.

Disappointment flashed across Suis's face. She grabbed the young girl and shoved her forward. "Dolly, take Dolly!"

The poor girl staggered to a stop in front of me, her eyes full of fear, her limbs shaking.

"What?"

"I trade Dolly for colset. She is good slave, Dolly!" Suis insisted.

"She's a slave?"

"I have many slaves. Very rich," she said, touching her chest proudly.

I was appalled. Indians owned slaves, too! Papa had very firm ideas about slavery. He was completely opposed to the practice and had raised me to believe the same. "It's indecent to own another human being, Janey," he always said.

"I'm terribly sorry, but I can't," I said.

Suis flushed red and then proceeded to yell at me in Chinook, no doubt something very disagreeable. Then she yelled at Dolly and stomped off in a huff, leaving the two of us to stare at her departing furious figure.

"Perhaps I should have given her the corset," I whispered.

Dolly said nothing, but her eyes seemed to agree with me.

By the time the sun was sinking over the mountains, my spirits were much improved.

I had bathed. I had brushed and pinned up my hair. I had

secured sleeping accommodations. Best of all, I had washed all my dresses and hung them to dry on the laundry line behind Mr. Russell's cabin. I would be able to put on a clean dress in the morning. I could hardly wait.

Now all I needed to do was find William.

Mr. Swan, Mr. Russell, Jehu, Captain Johnson, Father Joseph, and I gathered in the horrible little cabin at the rickety sawbuck table for supper. There was a bright fire in the hearth, and its warmth spread through my muscles, relaxing me. Mr. Swan ladled out a stew prepared by Mr. Russell. The stew contained potatoes, onions, and some sort of fish, and it was surprisingly agreeable. Then again, after the long weeks at sea, anything not full of weevils would have tasted agreeable to me.

Brandywine circled the table, wagging his tail and whining piteously for food. The wretched hound was not any kind of guard dog. By the sag of his plump belly, it was clear that he preferred eating to any kind of patrolling. "Here, beast," Mr. Russell said, tossing Brandywine a scrap.

Mr. Swan smiled fondly at the hound. "Brandywine feels obliged to eat as often as possible. He was the only survivor of the sloop *Brandywine*. She wrecked off the coast. We found him wandering the beach, thin and hungry."

"Life is short. Eat whenever you can, I always say," Jehu said. "There's nothing worse than an empty belly."

"We eat well here, my good man," Mr. Swan said. "The Chinooks are great traders and often trade with us for all manner of foodstuffs."

I remembered Dolly.

"Mr. Swan," I asked. "These Indians trade slaves?"

"Oh yes, indeed. Although *dentalia* is the principal currency."

"*Dentalia?*" I asked, trying the word out on my tongue.

"Shells. They use them in necklaces and such. The Chinooks call them *hiqua*." I recalled Suis's necklace.

"They enslave their own people?" Father Joseph asked in a shocked-sounding voice.

"No, my good man. They trade with other Indians along the coast. And of course they take slaves in battle or as blood prices for slain family members. Wealth is a sign of status, so owning slaves is a very serious business. The *tyee* is generally the wealthiest one in a particular village and so often owns the most slaves. The slaves are the ones with the round heads. The Chinooks have the flattened heads. You see—"

I was starting to think that Mr. Swan had flattened his head, the way he yammered on forever.

"Mr. Swan," I interrupted. "Where is William? I still don't understand why he isn't here."

"William is presently on a mission for Governor Stevens. He is involved in negotiating land treaties with the Indians of the territory."

"Territory?"

"Yes, my dear. We are our own territory now. The land north of the Columbia River has been declared the great Washington Territory."

"I see. But why is William involved with the Indians?" I

asked. "He wrote me that he had secured land here in Shoalwater Bay. I understood he was endeavoring to start a timber business?"

Mr. Swan sighed and removed his spectacles. He started to clean them with a grubby square of cloth that I supposed was his pocket-handkerchief. "Well, William had a bit of a problem with his claim."

"A problem?"

"I'm not exactly sure of the details. In any event William sought the advice of Governor Stevens, and the governor took a shine to your betrothed and hired him. The governor is trying to broker an agreement with the various tribes. A tricky proposition."

"Do you know where William is right now?"

"Generally, yes." He blinked owlishly at me.

"Where?"

"Somewhere to the north, I believe." A pause. "Or perhaps it was somewhere in the east? I'm afraid I don't quite remember," Mr. Swan said with an apologetic smile. "Have no fear. He'll turn up eventually. Everyone," he said expansively, "turns up eventually."

Captain Johnson belched loudly, interrupting. "Speaking of Indians, can I hire them on to help with the timber?"

Mr. Swan took a long draught of whiskey. "Oh yes, my good man. You'll have to stake a claim, of course."

That gave me an idea.

"Excuse me, Mr. Swan, about William—" But he was deep in conversation with Captain Johnson about hiring Indians to fell trees.

It was most frustrating. These men were clearly not used to the presence of a young lady. They could have all stood to read Rules of Conversation (Chapter Two), not to mention Deportment at the Dinner Table (Chapter Seven). Mr. Russell, in particular, was using his knife to pick his teeth in a most disgusting way and kept flicking little bits of food across the table.

"Yes, Miss Peck?" Mr. Swan said at last.

I leaned forward excitedly. "Would it be possible to hire an Indian, a messenger, to go and find William?"

He scratched his beard. "I suppose that would be possible."

"Do you think it would be expensive?" I had some money with me. Ten silver dollars. Papa had deposited funds for me at a bank in San Francisco, but it would not be easy to obtain access to it out here in the wilderness.

"The Chinooks live to trade, my dear, so I'm sure we'll be able to work something out."

"Thank you very much, Mr. Swan." I smiled at him in relief. There. It wasn't so terrible. I would simply send word to William that I was here, and he would return. Everything was going to work out in the end.

I sighed and leaned back in my chair. I gazed across the table, studying Jehu. He had a habit, I'd noticed, of crinkling his forehead when he was deep in thought.

"Capital meal, Mr. Russell." Mr. Swan added to this compliment a small burp and patted his round, full belly.

"Yes, that was very nice," I said, remembering my manners. "The fish stew was delicious."

"Wasn't fish," Mr. Russell said, continuing to pick his teeth with his knife.

"It wasn't? Then what was it?"

"Gull."

I swallowed hard. Surely I'd misheard him. "Gull?"

Mr. Russell glared at me. "Tasted good, dinnit?"

"Yes," I whispered.

"Then what ya complainin' about?"

Need I say how difficult it is to fall asleep when you have gull in your stomach?

Furthermore there was nothing soothing about the strange hoots and shrieks that echoed outside my tent. It was altogether different from the slapping sound of waves and creaking of the ship that had accompanied the nights at sea.

Something howled in the distance. I peered out the tent flaps. What if there was a beast like the one that had been hanging from the rafters of Mr. Russell's cabin waiting out there, ready to make a meal of a young girl?

I lay awake for what seemed a very great while, and I had just finally drifted off when I heard Brandywine barking wildly. After a moment, a loud shot rang through the night.

Someone was shooting right over my tent!

I cowered, frightened. Were we under attack by Indians? Was I going to be scalped after all?

Jehu's face appeared between the tent flaps.

"Jane, are you all right?"

I had never been so happy to see that scarred cheek.

"Yes," I whispered shakily, crawling out on hands and knees to see Handsome Jim aiming at the air above my tent with a rifle.

"*Memelose! Memelose!*" Handsome Jim shouted, pointing with the rifle to the air above the tent. Mr. Swan was staring at Handsome Jim, a bemused expression on his face.

"Mr. Swan, what is going on?" I demanded.

Mr. Swan chortled and swayed a little. Clearly the man had been drinking.

"Mr. Swan!"

He burst out laughing, and then tried to control himself.

Handsome Jim narrowed his eyes at Mr. Swan.

Mr. Swan wiped a tear of laughter from his cheek. "I'm afraid Handsome Jim is very superstitious. And, you see, my dear, I've been winding him up all night about *memeloses*. When Brandywine began barking outside, at our resident raccoon no doubt, I told Jim here that there was a *memelose* above your tent."

"Not funny, Swan," Handsome Jim growled, lowering his gun.

"I agree completely," I said, my eyes meeting Handsome Jim's.

Mr. Swan tried to look contrite. "I'm sorry, my dear. But we have so few amusements."

Handsome Jim glared at Mr. Swan and stalked off.

"It is hardly amusing. And if there *were* any spirits, they have most certainly been scared away on account of the racket," I muttered peevishly.

"D'urn gal, I can't speak for the spooks but you'd scare me

straight to blazes and I ain't even daid," Mr. Russell snorted, whiskers twitching.

"I didn't ask for your opinion, Mr. Russell," I said stiffly, putting a hand up to my unruly hair.

"The backs of the leaves are showing, gal," Mr. Russell declared cryptically. "You best come in the cabin now and not later."

I had no intention of listening to this overbearing, arrogant man. Miss Hepplewhite used to say that the only way to deal with men like him was to ignore them, and I intended to do just that.

"Mr. Russell, I stated very plainly that I would not be sleeping in that cabin. Now good night, sir."

"The cabin will—"

I pulled my tent flap shut with a firm snap. "Good night, Mr. Russell!"

Mr. Russell grumbled some more, and the men's voices drifted away.

Finally I would get some sleep after this long, dreadful day, I thought. I pulled the blanket up to my chin and, curling into a ball, fell asleep.

Next thing I knew, I was on the *Lady Luck*.

I was in our tiny cabin, and Mary's bunk was empty, the bedding neatly made up. All was quiet and still, except for the rhythmic slap of the waves.

Out of the stillness came a familiar scurrying sound. Hordes of rats began pouring into the room, leaping onto my bunk and biting me viciously. I screamed and screamed, but then the dream shifted, and all of a sudden I was on deck in the middle of a storm.

Massive waves slammed against the ship, rain pelted down in sheets, and I struggled to hold on to the rail. A flash of lightning crackled through the night, illuminating the inky ocean for one long heartbeat. And then I saw her.

Mary was standing on the deck, beneath the mainmast, still as a statue, her back to me, her black hair flowing like a waterfall.

"Mary!" I called.

But she didn't hear me. She just stood there, her pale skin glowing in the dark night.

I rushed across the deck, shouting her name over the wind. Then lightning struck the mainmast with a loud crack, and I watched in horror as the mast started to fall.

"Mary!" I screamed.

She turned around slowly and stared at me.

With dark, dead eyes.

I woke with a start, my heart pounding.

A crash of thunder rang through the night, and rain began pelting the tent.

"It was just a bad dream," I whispered to myself again and again.

The rain slapped noisily on the tent, and I wished with all my might that I was back in my four-poster bed on Walnut Street. Had I made a horrible mistake coming to this desolate place? Had I traded Papa and Mrs. Parker's cherry pie for a wilderness full of filthy men? Then I remembered William's beautiful eyes and lovely smile and knew that he was worth all these inconveniences. I would send a messenger for him first thing tomorrow, I promised myself. As soon as he found out I was in the territory, he would come for me directly, and all would be well.

I felt a stinging rush of cold water under my backside and looked down in alarm.

"Oh blast," I whispered softly.

Before I could move, a great wind came up, flapping the tent wildly. In the next moment the tent was gone, and I was left crouching over a small stream of water.

Entirely discouraged, I heaved up the sodden skirt of my woolen nightgown and made a dash for the dreaded cabin. I entertained little hope that anyone would be up, but when I opened the door a cheery fire was blazing and the men were sitting around drinking whiskey and laughing. They were all snug and dry. Brandywine was curled up in front of the fire. Even the sorry hound had known enough to get in from the storm.

Mr. Russell took in my wet nightdress and cackled. "Backs of the leaves, gal."

"I beg your pardon?"

"The backs of the leaves show when it's gonna rain, gal," Mr. Russell said, puffing on his pipe.

"You *knew* it was going to rain?" I asked incredulously.

"Could be I did."

"You—you—"

"You're most welcome to stay here, Miss Peck," Mr. Swan

interrupted, stepping between me and Mr. Russell and proffering a grimy wool blanket.

I didn't have much choice in the matter. I snatched the blanket and stalked over to the fire with as much dignity as I could muster. Every bunk contained a lumpy man, so I swiftly stripped out of my soggy nightdress under the blanket and bundled on the dirt floor next to the warm flames. The wool blanket smelled as if it had been used to clean a horse. I was utterly humiliated.

Brandywine lifted his head and gave a halfhearted sniff to see if I had brought any food.

"Worthless hound," I muttered.

I lay there wrapped in the grimy blanket on the filthy dirt floor with the sounds of snoring men filling my ears, and it all suddenly seemed too much. Mary was dead, Papa was far away, and William was missing. I was cold, wet, and naked. And I didn't have a friend in the world. Hot tears wet my cheeks as I cried my frustration and fear into the scratchy wool blanket.

I was just beginning to fall asleep when I felt someone lay another blanket on me. And a voice—was it Mr. Russell's?—said, "She sure is a stubborn gal."

CHAPTER EIGHT
or,
Dress as a Test of Character

I awoke early and crept out of the cabin to fetch one of my dresses. It had stopped raining sometime during the night. If I were lucky, my dresses would be merely damp and not soaking wet.

The sky was gray and grim, and the air smelled muddy. I couldn't help but notice that the roof of Mr. Russell's cabin was sprouting moss, which seemed to me a very bad sign. It must rain a considerable amount for moss to grow on one's roof.

I saw the abomination the minute I rounded the corner.

I did what any young lady would do. I screamed.

Handsome Jim came running out of the cabin, rifle at the ready no doubt expecting to find me in mortal danger.

"Shoot it!" I ordered, pointing at the perpetrator.

The cow regarded me with lazy eyes. She was calmly chewing away, a lace-trimmed hem hanging out of the corner of her mouth.

"Shoot cow?" Handsome Jim asked, confused.

I stamped my foot. "Yes. Shoot the blasted beast!"

Handsome Jim looked worried. "That cow Mr. Russell's. Burton!"

"I don't care! Just shoot the wretched animal!" I stamped my foot again.

Jehu emerged from the cabin, looking sleepy. He was shirtless, and his hair was mussed. "What's all the carrying-on?"

"Look!" I shrieked.

"And good morning to you, too, Miss Peck," Jehu said dryly.

I pointed angrily at the cow, which was methodically chewing, apparently unperturbed by the sight of a man holding a gun pointed in its general direction.

"That blasted beast ate all my dresses!"

Jehu started to laugh.

"It's not funny! What am I to wear?" I cried. The blanket slipped, and I gripped it tightly around me. What an unseemly predicament!

"I'm sure a lady like you will figure it out," Jehu said, and, still laughing, walked away.

I stared grimly into the smoldering fire. I had reluctantly put on my nightdress even though it was still wet from the night before. It was itchy and smelled rancid, like the inside of the cabin, but worse somehow. The only other dress I possessed was my wedding dress and I was not about to traipse around in that. It would be destroyed in no time. Above all, that must be saved for William.

"What am I to wear?"

"Why don't you ask Suis to trade one of hers?" Mr. Swan suggested mildly.

I remembered Miss Hepplewhite's counsel on Dress as a Test of Character (Chapter Eight):

Your true character is shown in your dress, girls.

"Mr. Swan, those dresses are immodest!"

He shrugged good-naturedly. "The Chinook ladies seem comfortable enough."

"But Suis goes around practically naked! Why, you can see her—her ankles!—in that dress she wears!"

"Her ankles, you say?" Mr. Swan rubbed his chin thoughtfully.

As if she knew I was speaking of her, Suis appeared in the doorway of the cabin, carrying a bundle. Clearly Handsome Jim had related the situation to her and she had come, ready to bargain.

"Guess I'll leave you ladies to it." Mr. Swan winked knowingly and disappeared outside.

Suis undid the bundle and held out a skirt similar to the one she was wearing and a calico blouse.

A little girl peeked out at me from behind Suis's legs.

"But what can I trade?" I asked plaintively.

Suis poked me in the ribs, pushing the whalebones of my corset into my side. I inhaled sharply.

"My corset?" I asked in dismay.

She nodded inexorably. "Trade colset."

I had worn a corset for so long, I didn't know what to do without one. What would Miss Hepplewhite say? Furthermore, what would William say when he returned and saw me? What kind of respectable young lady went about dressed like an Indian?

A dry one, whispered a voice that sounded suspiciously like Papa's.

The skirt and blouse she held looked so clean and dry. Something in me relented.

"Very well," I said reluctantly.

Suis smiled smugly.

I unlaced the corset, leaving on my drawers and shift, and slipped into the calico blouse, my petticoats, and the Chinook skirt. The skirt was a series of woven strands of some material that created a thick fringe and left my legs exposed below the knee. It smelled sweet and it was heaven to be dry.

"It is cedar," Suis said, indicating my skirt. "Beaten soft."

I could hardly believe I was wearing a tree, but clearly I was.

Despite myself, I smiled. It felt, well, *nice* not to have the corset on. It was somehow easier to breathe. Perhaps Papa was right about corsets, after all.

The little girl tugged on my hand shyly. I knelt down.

"And what is your name?"

"Sootie," Suis said with obvious pride.

The little girl grinned, exposing missing front teeth. She had a slanted forehead like her mother, and wide, curious brown eyes.

"It means 'mouse,'" Suis explained.

"Is she your daughter?"

Suis nodded, smoothing her daughter's hair back.

I had not yet put up my hair, and it hung loose in a tangle of curls. Sootie reached out and touched it in wonder, pulling her hands through it as if to assure herself it was real.

"Have you never seen red hair?" I asked with a laugh as the little girl's fingers caught and tugged through the mass.

A sudden image of Mary combing my hair as I sat at my bedroom table at Walnut Street flashed before my eyes, and for a fleeting moment the feel of those gentle fingers brought back a rush of memories so fierce all I could do was blink.

Mr. Swan was waiting for me on the porch when we emerged from the cabin.

"You look much improved, my dear," Mr. Swan said brightly.

"She looks beautiful," a voice said admiringly.

Jehu was leaning against the porch.

I shifted awkwardly in my new outfit. How strange it felt to be in public without a corset! I had to force myself not to cross my arms in front of my bosom. As if sensing my discomfort, Father Joseph appeared at that very moment and frowned at me.

"That ensemble is hardly appropriate for a decent Christian girl," he said sternly.

I felt like perishing on the spot.

Mr. Swan came to my rescue. He cleared his throat loudly. "Come, Miss Peck. We have an errand requiring all haste," he said, waving a sturdy-looking walking stick importantly.

I looked at him blankly for a moment, then realizing his game, said, "Oh yes! We must hurry." I was anxious to be away from

Father Joseph's admonishments, even if the sky was gray and it was starting to drizzle.

Mr. Swan's eyes crinkled softly in understanding.

I followed Mr. Swan as he trampled down the stream to where a strange-looking collection of buildings was situated. There were Indians everywhere: women laughing, small children running and playing, men chattering away to each other.

"This is Toke's village," he said. "Those are the lodges."

"Mr. Swan, I need to secure a messenger, to send word to William," I reminded him.

"Of course, my dear."

I followed him over to one of the long wooden lodges.

"How do we get in?" I asked, looking for a door but seeing none.

"Through here," Mr. Swan said, disappearing through a small opening near the ground, a sort of rabbit's hole but big enough to fit a person.

I slipped after him into the dark hole, and I fairly gasped in astonishment at the scene before me.

The room was massive, and firepits lining the center bustled with activity. There were women preparing salmon, babies being cared for by their mothers, and men engaged in a fierce game of some kind. Dolly smiled shyly at me from the corner where she appeared to be weaving a basket.

Huge bunklike structures, platforms really, were arrayed against the walls, and it was perfectly astonishing to see whole families perched on these platforms observing us with great interest. It appeared that several families lived in Chief Toke's large lodge. What was most astounding was that the lodge was so clean and tidy. The floors were lined with mats, and it all smelled sweetly of cedar. Mr. Russell's cabin seemed positively a pigsty in comparison.

Chief Toke was sitting on a platform at the end of the room. When he saw Mr. Swan, he gestured to us. Mr. Swan explained my situation to him, and in short order we were discussing my needs with a young man.

"This is Yelloh. He is one of Chief Toke's nephews. He is acquainted with William and says that he has a fair idea of where he might be," Mr. Swan said.

Yelloh had a ring made from a shell in his nose. I couldn't stop looking at it.

"Does he speak English?" I whispered.

"I'm afraid that Yelloh does not. Most of the Indians prefer to speak the Jargon when communicating with whites or other tribes. It's much more practical. Although, I must say, some of the Indians, like Suis and Handsome Jim, speak English quite well. The children seem to speak English the best. But you should really learn the Jargon, my dear. It is a fascinating language."

It was becoming clear to me that Mr. Swan was very fond of giving lectures. "Will they take American money?" I asked.

"Of course, my dear."

"How much?"

Mr. Swan spoke to Yelloh and then turned back to me. "Five silver dollars."

"Five dollars?" I asked, aghast. That was half my funds!

"He says five silver dollars for fifteen days' travel north and fifteen travel back. A month, to be clear. If he does not find William in that time he will come back. You must make him a counteroffer, my dear," Mr. Swan said.

I needed to make my ten dollars last.

"Tell him three dollars for ten days in each direction."

Mr. Swan translated, and Yelloh shook his head.

"He says that he heard from a cousin that William has gone very far north, and that it will take him at least twelve days. His final price is four silver dollars."

I looked at Mr. Swan anxiously.

He smiled apologetically. "My dear, I do believe that William has traveled a considerable distance."

"Very well," I said. "Four dollars for twelve days each way." I handed him the money. "Do not go a day over twelve days."

Mr. Swan related my concern to Yelloh. The young man inclined his head gravely.

"He promises to travel twelve days only."

I looked suspiciously at Yelloh.

Mr. Swan nodded reassuringly. "Have no fear. Chief Toke says he is very capable."

I was having a hard time considering anyone who had a ring in his nose as capable of much of anything. The fellow couldn't even sneeze. How could he find William?

"Is he trustworthy?" I asked.

"I confess I don't know him very well, but he seems a nice enough lad to me."

It wasn't as if I had much of a choice. "Very well."

Mr. Swan grinned at Yelloh, who nodded.

"Now that that's resolved, why don't we make our way down to the beach?" Mr. Swan suggested cheerily, as if it were an ordinary day and we were setting out to call on a neighbor.

I tromped after him along a narrow trail. It was drizzling harder now, but Mr. Swan seemed not the least bit bothered. I could feel my hair start to escape from its knot. My hair was at its worst in wet weather.

"Does it rain very much here?" I asked.

"Nearly always, my dear girl."

I was doomed.

"Except, of course, in the summer, when it is quite beautiful. Just wait until July," he promised.

We made our way down to the dark sandy beach, where a large canoe rested. It was the same canoe Mr. Swan had met us in the day we'd arrived.

"That's mine. Isn't she a beauty?"

I judged the canoe to be nearly thirty feet long. It looked as if it could carry a dozen people. There was a carved head of a bird on its prow, and it was painted black on the outside and red on the inside. It was indeed quite impressive.

"Toke traded it to me. It was carved from a single cedar tree. Can you imagine?" He shook his head in wonderment. "It took more than three months to make. And look, those are little snail shells embedded as decoration. Simply marvelous workmanship."

He reminded me of the way Papa talked when he was excited

about an interesting case. Except, of course, Mr. Swan wasn't a surgeon. In fact, I wasn't at all certain what his occupation was.

"Mr. Swan, why are you here?" I asked.

"I am chronicling these Indians, Jane," he said. He drew out a small diary from his pocket. "I write down my observations on the Indians and their customs and their languages. And then of course there is the flora and fauna of the region, which is distinct and worth studying."

It seemed a bit mad.

"Yes, but how could you leave civilization for this?" I said. We were standing on the edge of the beach. The horizon was slate gray, the air damp. The trees in the distance rose high and thick. It was all so wild; I longed to see something familiar and civilized, like a proper roof or a cobblestone street.

Mr. Swan took a deep breath and gestured widely. "How could I not? This is the *frontier*, Jane. History is being made all around us, and we are in the thick of it."

Something stirred in me at his words, something that reminded me of Jebediah Parker and the enthusiasm of a young boy.

"We are living in exciting times," he insisted, waving a hand. The sun caught his hand and something glinted on his finger. It was a slender gold band. I felt a rush of sympathy for the unfortunate man. No doubt he had come out to escape the memory of his poor dead wife.

"But Mr. Swan," I said. "You will not meet another woman out here in these wilds."

"Why would I want to meet another woman?"

"Isn't your wife dead?"

"My wife—dead? No, she is very much alive, as are my two children."

I shook my head, bewildered. "But where are they?"

His eyes clouded. "Boston."

"Really! Well, when shall they be joining you out here?" I asked eagerly. It would be so cheering to have the company of another lady in this wilderness.

He sighed heavily. "They aren't. Matilda does not wish to come," he said, and I was startled by the sorrow in his voice.

"But why?"

"She is a lady," he said shortly.

"I am a lady," I said defensively. There was something about the way he said it that sounded like an accusation. The wind brushed against my bare legs, and I looked at my Chinook skirt. "Or I used to be."

"Of course you are, Miss Peck. But an altogether different sort of lady, I suspect, than my wife."

I didn't know whether or not I should be offended, although I imagined that his wife had made the correct decision. There were bathtubs in Boston, not to mention respectable dresses. And wasn't it just a bit odd to abandon one's wife and children to study Indians?

We passed a group of Chinook women weaving baskets industriously, and all at once I stopped.

"Mr. Swan, what am I to do until William arrives?"

"What did you do before you came here?"

"I attended Miss Hepplewhite's Young Ladies Academy."

"How interesting." He rubbed his beard thoughtfully. "And what were you studying? Mathematics? Philosophy? History? Botany?"

"Etiquette, Embroidery, Watercolors, Music, and I had just begun Conversational French when I left," I said. "In fact, it was William's good suggestion that I attend in the first place."

"I see," Mr. Swan said.

"I was an excellent student."

Mr. Swan looked at me, his spectacles gleaming in the sun. He had the same expression Papa had when I told him about Miss Hepplewhite's.

"I imagine you were."

"Well?" I asked. "What am I to do?"

"I suppose you'll just muddle along, like the rest of us," Mr. Swan said with a jolly smile.

And then he started walking on again.

That evening Chief Toke invited us to supper at his lodge in honor of our arrival.

Mr. Swan rubbed his hands together. "You are in for a real treat, my dear."

The floor of the lodge was a hive of activity with supper being prepared. The air inside was smoky from all the cooking and for a moment my eyes stung, but then they adjusted to the dim interior. There were no windows, and it seemed strangely darker than it had during my earlier visit. I looked up and saw stars glittering through spaces between the cedar planks that served as the roof. Below the ceiling, a grid of poles had been rigged, upon which fish were laid.

"Mr. Swan, why are there fish hanging from the roof?" I asked.

"That is how they preserve the salmon, with the smoke," Mr. Swan said.

Without any hesitation, Mr. Swan scrambled up onto one of the benches arrayed along the length of the lodge, and after a moment I did the same, followed by Jehu. It was considerably easier to climb in my new skirt. Nevertheless Father Joseph shook his head when he saw my bare ankles.

"Mademoiselle," he muttered under his breath.

Sootie caught sight of me and quickly climbed up to show off her doll. It seemed to be little more than a clam shell dressed in a scrap of fabric, but I knew she loved it by the way she hugged it so tightly. I suddenly remembered the rag doll Papa had sewn for me when I was a small girl. I had carried that little doll with me everywhere until finally her yarn hair had fallen off and both arms went missing.

"You loved that doll to death," Papa had said with a smile, shaking his head at my poor armless doll.

I pictured the lovely dining room in our house on Walnut Street and wondered what Papa was having for supper. Most likely Mrs. Parker's roast pork and apples, I thought with a pang. She always cooked roast pork and apples on Thursdays. At least, I thought it was Thursday.

Our supper consisted of freshly caught salmon and some

strange roasted root vegetables. After the gull incident, I resolved it was better not to ask. I looked around. Although there were rough-looking bowls with carved spoons, there were no forks or knives in sight.

Mr. Swan winked. "You must use your fingers, my dear."

Heavens! People of polite society simply did not use their fingers, but my belly was growling in a most determined way. In my fuss with the dress that morning, breakfast had been forgotten. All the others seemed to be using their fingers. What would Miss Hepplewhite say?

My belly growled loudly.

Jehu heard it and laughed. "Better eat, Miss Peck."

Gingerly I picked up a piece of fish and put it in my mouth as quickly as I could.

The salmon melted on my tongue. It was delicious. In short order my salmon was gone, and my fingers were sticky. Deportment at the Dinner Table (Chapter Seven) advised that a handkerchief could be used in a pinch if a napkin could not be found, but I had neither. I glanced around, and then, when I was positive no one was looking, quickly licked my fingers.

"You should've brought one of those embroidered hankies," Jehu said.

I blushed at being caught.

A moment later a bowl of water was passed around the room to clean our fingers. It seemed that the Indians had their own version of proper table manners after all. Although Mr. Russell, gentleman that he was, preferred to use his sleeve instead.

"I'm taking some of my boys and looking for a timber claim tomorrow, Swan," Captain Johnson boomed.

"Very good, Captain," Mr. Swan said.

A flicker of apprehension shot through me. I turned to Jehu. "Will you be joining the captain?" I did not want to be abandoned with only Father Joseph for company.

He shook his head. "I'm staying here to make repairs on the *Lady Luck*."

I nodded, unaccountably relieved.

Brandywine was snoring lightly by one of the fires, his belly full of food. Chief Toke eyed the sleeping dog and said something in the Jargon. Everyone laughed.

"Toke says that dog, he have salmon for *Tomanawos*," Handsome Jim explained to me.

"What's *Tomanawos*?"

"Chinook people, we all have *Tomanawos*," he said.

"And what is that exactly?"

Mr. Swan explained. "The Chinook believe that every person has his own guardian spirit, or *Tomanawos*, that watches over him. It's usually an animal, like a bear or an eagle or some such. This guardian spirit protects and guides them."

"Spirits?" Father Joseph asked, his fuzzy eyebrows arching.

"Yes, my good man. The Chinook are great believers in spirits," Mr. Swan said.

I turned to Handsome Jim. "What is your *Tomanawos*?"

Handsome Jim shook his head. "Secret." He regarded me with interest. "Boston Jane, you have *Tomanawos*?"

"No." Clearly I had no guardian spirit looking after me. If I did, I would never have been in this muddle in the first place.

Across the campfire, Chief Toke's sharp eyes bored into mine. He said something and everyone around the fire laughed, except Suis, who looked startled.

"What?" I asked nervously. "What did he say?"

"Boston Jane, she have *Tomanawos* because she looks more beautiful in Chinook dress," Handsome Jim said, beaming.

Chief Toke spoke again and then grinned at me.

Mr. Russell hooted with laughter.

Suis's eyes darted back and forth between the men, her face hardening.

"Now what did he say?" It was terribly frustrating not being able to understand this Jargon, and I had a bad feeling they were amusing themselves at my expense.

"Toke says that you are much better off in the Chinook style of dress than your Boston dress. Now you can run freely like the elk," Mr. Swan said.

"Ladies do not run," I said firmly.

Handsome Jim rapidly translated for Chief Toke. Chief Toke looked as if he felt sorry for me.

"Toke ask Boston Jane, why she not want to run like elk?" Handsome Jim translated.

"Or kick your heels up and dance?" Jehu added softly.

"Dance?" I whispered in a shocked voice.

"That's a dress meant for dancing," Jehu said. His eyes seemed to glow in the firelight.

I held up my hand, as if to ward away the very idea. Miss Hepplewhite was firmly opposed to dancing.

"Dancing is a wicked pursuit," Father Joseph said, as if seconding Miss Hepplewhite's long-ago opinion. "And not fit for a good Christian girl."

Jehu shook his head in disappointment.

Chief Toke smiled at me and said something that made Handsome Jim grin wildly.

Handsome Jim started to translate. "Toke says that Boston Jane have—"

Suis interrupted loudly, her voice strident. "Boston Jane, she not have *Tomanawos. Boston tillicums,* they do not have *Tomanawos.*"

Chief Toke looked at Suis sharply, but Suis just glared at him.

It didn't seem like a good idea to make an enemy of the chief's wife, so I hastened to agree. "You're right, of course. I don't have a *Tomanawos.*"

"Boston Jane, she not have *Tomanawos!*" she insisted, looking right at me.

Sootie looked on with wide eyes, clearly upset by her mother's shouting.

Chief Toke barked something at her, but Suis got up and stalked away.

I threw up my hands in bewilderment. "What did I do?"

"I don't know," Jehu said. "But you sure do have a way with people."

CHAPTER NINE
or,
Pouring Tea and Coffee

I was situated on the beach, working on a rather dismal watercolor of the bay, when it became clear that I needed less color and more gray.

It had rained every day since our arrival. I went about in a constant state of sogginess. My hair was an eternally tangled, wild mess in this weather. I was grateful Sally Biddle was on the other side of the continent, for I could almost hear her comparing my hair to a squirrel's nest.

Watercolors were not my strong suit, but Miss Hepplewhite had very kindly given me a small supply of paints and paper and brushes as a wedding present, and I was determined to paint a picture for William. Besides, it was a way to pass the time. I had rigged my parasol over my easel to protect it from the rain, but the wind shifted and a fine spray spattered the paper, causing the paint to run.

"Blast!" I whispered to myself, trying to mop off the water without smearing the landscape.

"Yar going to have to start working for yar grub, gal!" a voice said loudly.

I nearly jumped out of my skin.

Mr. Russell stood behind me with an obstinate look on his face. He spat a huge wad of tobacco. It landed on the sand next to my shoe.

"You scared me to death," I said, hand fluttering to my chest.

"Like I said, gal, yar gonna have to pitch in. What can ya do?"

"I am very skilled at supervising help," I explained reasonably. Miss Hepplewhite had always stressed the importance of running a good household, with particular emphasis on managing help politely but firmly. I could also make very good flower arrangements.

Mr. Russell snorted.

"Ain't no *help* here, gal."

"But what about the Indians?" I asked. There were always Indians in and about Mr. Russell's cabin.

He shook his head. "Not 'less ya got money to pay 'em."

I needed to keep my money to find William.

"What would you have me do?" I stared at him peevishly.

"Can ya sew?"

"I'm quite skilled at embroidery. I took first place at Miss Hepplewhite's Young Ladies Academy for my embroidery of a violet on a pocket-handkerchief!" I announced proudly.

One of his long whiskers jerked.

"Follow me," he grunted, and he turned sharply, striding rapidly up the beach. I abandoned my easel and followed, perplexed, until we arrived at the cabin.

He pointed to a towering pile of rags in the corner.

"Thar's the mending," he announced. From the top of the heap he grabbed a crusty-looking pair of pants with a considerable tear in the seat. "I 'specially need my pants fixed. Thar the only other pair I got besides the ones I'm wearing."

"You expect me to repair those filthy things?" I asked, appalled.

Wasn't it enough that I had to sleep in this horrid cabin, being kept awake by snoring men night after night? Father Joseph was the worst. He snored loud enough to be heard back in Philadelphia. Not to mention, my blankets were festooned with fleas, worse than the bunks on the ship. Miss Hepplewhite said that a good guest never complained but truly, I was on the verge of losing my composure. Between the fleas and the snoring, I barely got a minute's rest.

And now I was expected to mend their awful clothes as if I were little more than a common maid. Did they truly expect me to *be* the help?

"Ain't good for much, are ya?" Mr. Russell said, shaking his head disdainfully.

I was seized by a sudden longing to prove him wrong.

"I can sew a small stitch and a straight seam more perfectly than you deserve," I said. I'd show the horrible man!

I snatched the filthy pants and marched away.

It took me nearly all afternoon to mend Mr. Russell's pants.

Naturally I had to wash them first as they were so utterly filthy. Mr. Russell must have fought off an entire herd of wild animals in them for all the holes they bore. Believe me when I say that I was greatly tempted to embroider a violet on the backside.

I presented the pants to him, clean and mended.

He grunted.

Mr. Russell rapidly became the bane of my existence.

The only thing the mountain man was skilled at was tearing his clothes to bits. No matter how much mending I did, the pile in the corner never seemed any smaller.

And then one morning I discovered Champ, one of the odd assortment of the dozen pioneers who lived in the settlement, lurking around the cabin. Men were continually coming and going from Mr. Russell's cabin, as it served as the only trading post on the entire bay. Champ was notable for his ratty-looking beard. It was overgrown and greatly resembled a scraggly broom.

"What are you doing?" I asked indignantly.

Champ took off his hat. "Well, ma'am, I jest need this here shirt fixed. It's got a powerful tear on the back."

"Did Mr. Russell inform you that you could put your mending in this pile?"

"No," he said sheepishly. And then added, "But he didn't say I couldn't."

"How long has this been going on?"

"I don't know." He cleared his throat. "But all the boys been putting their clothes here!"

"All the boys?" I whispered dangerously.

"Near as I can figure."

"You mean . . . to tell me . . . that I have been doing . . . the mending . . . for *all* the filthy men of Shoalwater Bay?" I asked slowly.

The man blanched.

"Kindly inform *all the boys* that I will not be doing any more mending! Do you understand?"

Champ nodded, shamefaced.

I stomped around the cabin and confronted Mr. Russell where he was milking his loathsome cow.

"Mr. Russell!" I stamped my foot.

His eyes flicked over, acknowledging me.

"Did you know that every pioneer in this territory has been putting his mending in that pile?"

"Might have."

"I am not a maid!"

"Ya can sew and wash, can't ya?"

"I am a lady, and I will only do mending for you and Mr. Swan. Is that clear?"

He shrugged, spat a wad of tobacco, and went back to milking.

It wasn't until I was back in the cabin that I noticed the glob of tobacco sticking wetly to the tip of my shoe.

"Blasted man," I muttered.

Yelloh had been gone for a week and I had not received a word of his progress. Then a second week passed.

Then a third.

I grew more frustrated at my situation, but there was little I could do but bide my time in this increasingly grim country. It rained nearly every day, a gray, drizzly mist that seeped into my skin and made me feel altogether detestable. It proved entirely impossible to keep my shoes dry. I began to understand why the Indians went about barefoot. The weather made such uncivilized behavior seem civilized.

After supper one evening, Mr. Russell said, "How 'bout some coffee, gal?"

If there was one thing I could do, it was pour coffee!

"I'd be delighted to pour the coffee," I said, remembering the helpful hints from Pouring Tea and Coffee (Chapter Three). As there were no children present, I wouldn't have to worry about the strength of it, and Miss Hepplewhite always said that men preferred coffee with just a spoonful of sugar.

"Not just pour it, gal," Mr. Russell said. "Ya gotta make it, too."

"Make it?"

"It don't make itself." His whiskers twitched. "Ya do know how to make coffee, don't ya, gal?"

The men were all staring at me as if I were stupid. Was I really so ignorant as not to know how to make such a simple thing?

I pulled myself up. "Of course I do."

He grunted.

In actual fact Mrs. Parker or Mary had always been the ones to make the coffee and I had been the one to pour it, but how difficult could it be? I went over to the shelves where Mr. Russell kept the supplies and found the tin of coffee beans. Sitting on a lower shelf were salt, cinnamon, peppercorns, and sugar. Behind the peppercorns was a grinder. Easy enough.

"Don't forget to clean the grinder, gal," Mr. Russell ordered.

The grinder was already coated a thick black. Clearly cleaning it was not something that was usual to the routine of making coffee. I nodded, but I had no intention of being ordered about any more than necessary by that man.

I poured some beans into the grinder, ground them up well, and then added them to the coffeepot to boil. I set out tin cups and had the milk and sugar at the ready. After the coffee was well boiled, I poured it into the cups, added milk and sugar, and brought everything to the table.

Mr. Swan smiled appreciatively. "It smells lovely, my dear."

He took a hearty swallow. His eyes bulged in shock and immediately began to water.

Jehu, who had taken a swallow at the same time, started to choke. He knocked over his chair and ran for the door.

Father Joseph spewed his coffee across the table and started coughing violently. He clutched his mouth, shot me a look of horror, and also ran out of the cabin.

Handsome Jim stared at his coffee with trepidation.

"Dang gal, what are ya trying to do? Kill us?" Mr. Russell shouted. He was red in the face from coughing. He threw his tin cup at the cabin wall. It landed with a bang.

"I don't understand!"

"Thar's pepper in this here coffee!"

I heard someone retching outside.

"Pepper?" I sniffed at a cup. It *did* smell slightly of pepper. "But how did it get there?"

"The grinder, gal! Ya got to clean the grinder! How do ya think we get pepper?"

"How was I to know it was pepper?" I asked, throwing my hands up.

He sneezed loudly.

"Everyone knows, gal! Everyone 'cept you because yar so dang useless!"

"I am not useless!"

"Ya are! Yar plain useless!" he roared, and then let out a tremendous sneeze right in my face.

Can you imagine my humiliation? I stormed out of the wretched cabin and marched down to the beach. I stared miserably out at the bay, at the *Lady Luck* anchored there, my mind working furiously. It had never been my intention to come west so that I could become maid to a gang of unruly men! They were ungrateful, ungracious louts, every last one of them!

Jehu followed me down to the beach. His eyes were still watering.

"You sure can pour a cup of coffee," he said dryly.

"He is the most horrible man in the world!" I burst out. "I hate him! And I am not useless. I can do many things. Why, I can embroider and paint watercolors and pour tea and coffee and I know how to manage a household and arrange flowers and send out invitations and—"

Jehu stared at me silently.

"It's not my fault I don't know how to cook!" I cried. "That was Mary's job!"

"Jane," Jehu said patiently. "This isn't Philadelphia. I know it's hard, but Mr. Russell's right. You have to pitch in."

"I already do the mending," I said stubbornly.

"Yes," he said. "But who do you think chops the wood, and milks the cow, and catches the fish, and cleans the fire, and every other little thing that needs doing? Everyone works. There aren't any servants here. The least you could do is help with the meals."

"But I don't know how to cook!"

He looked me in the eye and said, "Then learn."

Yelloh appeared at first light. It was not a minute too soon.

It had been a terrible night in Mr. Russell's cabin. The men had been up coughing and sneezing from the pepper, and Mr. Russell had been the worst. Between coughing fits he had muttered, "Dang useless gal."

I was sitting on the horrible little porch darning a sock when Yelloh appeared. At the grim look on his face, my heart fell.

"Where's William?" I demanded, fearing the worst. "Has something happened to William? Why isn't he with you?"

Yelloh shook his head. He had no idea what I was saying. I looked about for help.

"Handsome Jim!" I waved him over.

Handsome Jim greeted Yelloh, and the two began speaking in Chinook.

"Handsome Jim," I broke in. "Ask him where William is."

He nodded and spoke to Yelloh.

"Yelloh says he miss Boston William by two days," Handsome Jim explained.

"Blast it! But why didn't he go after William?" I asked wildly.

"Yelloh says Boston Jane tell him twelve days only."

I looked at Yelloh in frustration. "But William was so close!"

"Yelloh says Boston Jane tell him twelve days only," Handsome Jim said seriously. "Yelloh, he is very good man. He not cheat you."

I shook my head at the ridiculousness of it.

"Ask him if he knows where William is now."

Handsome Jim turned to Yelloh, who said emphatically, "*Narwitka!*" The ring in his nose swung slightly.

"Certainly," Handsome Jim beamed.

"Where?"

The two men conferred.

"Well?" I demanded.

"Very far," Handsome Jim said.

"How far?"

"A month."

A month! It had cost me four silver dollars to have him travel twelve days. I would never be able to afford a whole month in each direction!

I ran into the cabin and rummaged in my chest. I ran back out and thrust my six silver dollars into Yelloh's hand.

"This is all the money I have! Will you please find him?" I pleaded.

Yelloh hesitated and looked at Handsome Jim.

Handsome Jim murmured something softly. I pressed the silver coins into Yelloh's hand.

"Please," I begged.

After a moment he nodded, and I felt the breath go out of me in relief.

Handsome Jim looked at Yelloh and back to me. "He find Boston William."

A month out and a month back.

It was nearly June, and I was going to be stranded here well past July by the looks of things. Two more months of horrid Mr. Russell, who had not forgiven me for the coffee incident. And then there was Suis. The Chinook woman glared at me every time she saw me. I had clearly offended her in some way but knew not how.

It was awful. Time passed so slowly here without Mary. The voyage on the ship had been terrible, but at least Mary and I had had each other for company.

To cheer myself up, I had taken William's old letters and gone down to the bay to sit under my parasol in the drizzling rain and reread them. I knew William would want me to be brave, but Shoalwater Bay was such a disagreeable place that just thinking about it put me in a grim mood.

Not to mention I had received no letters from Papa. Of course, I knew this was too much to expect, as insufficient time had passed for him to have even received my first letter, let alone respond to it. Assuming, of course, that my missive had not been routed via the China Sea.

I had written Papa upon my arrival saying that we'd landed, and I was well, and the sad news about Mary. But I had been careful to avoid mentioning William. I could not bear the thought of having to inform Papa that William was missing. It

would merely serve to confirm his poor opinion of William. I would wait, I decided, until William had returned and we were wed, to send Papa a second letter.

With a sigh I got up and started back to the dreary cabin.

As I walked along the path, something orange-red caught my eye.

Cherries?

No, the strange berry resembled a blackberry except it had an unusual orange-red color.

A sudden image of Mrs. Parker's cherry pie came to me.

Mr. Swan was sitting at the sawbuck table scribbling in his diary when I returned to the cabin.

"Mr. Swan, do you know what this is?" I asked, holding out the small berry.

"Hello, my dear." He peered over the rim of his glasses. "That is a salmonberry. I am particularly fond of them myself."

"Do you think I could make a pie with them?"

Mr. Swan looked very uncomfortable. "I suppose it is possible to make a pie using salmonberries," he said hesitantly, as if to say, it's very possible for someone to make a pie using salmonberries, just not you, my dear.

The look on his face made me more determined than ever.

Now I just needed to figure out how to make a pie. I had vague memories of Mrs. Parker making her cherry pie, but memories would not do. Jehu knew how to cook, I remembered, thinking of the chicken broth he had once made for Mary. Perhaps he could help.

I found him on the beach, supervising the sailors as they cut a piece of timber for the new mainmast on the *Lady Luck*. He stopped what he was doing when he saw me and walked over.

A sliver of sunshine broke out from behind the clouds, sending light dancing across the smooth bay.

"Do you know how to make a pie?" I asked.

"Why?" He squinted into the sun.

"I found some salmonberries. I thought I'd try to make one, only I don't know how."

"Don't know how to make one myself."

I stared at him in disappointment. I was so sure he would know.

"Did you say Mary was a cook?" he asked.

"Yes. She wanted to open a boardinghouse here and cook for the men."

"Maybe she had some receipts in her things. Cooks I know like to write these things down."

I ran all the way back to the cabin. I had put Mary's things in my trunk after she died. She'd brought a small sack with her, and I hadn't been able to bring myself to look inside it before, but I did now. Her possessions spilled out on the sawbuck table. An apron, well-used wooden spoons, a rolling pin, a thick piece of cloth that smelled of flour, a pot, a pie plate, and a small diary.

I paged carefully through the diary, which wasn't really a diary at all. It was a collection of receipts. Biscuits and gravy. Fricasseed chicken. Roasted pork and apples. My mouth watered just reading the words. Sponge cake. Rice custard. Bird's nest pudding. Lemon drops. Fritters. Doughnuts. Gingerbread. And . . .

Mrs. Parker's Cherry Pie!

"Take half a peck of cherries . . ."

As I read the receipt I could almost hear Papa's deep laugh, smell Mrs. Parker's kitchen, feel the warmth of the stove. It was all so very far away. As far away as Mary, at the bottom of the cold, dark ocean. I closed my eyes, clutching the small, dear book to my heart.

I couldn't bring her back, but I could do one thing.

I could make a pie.

Mr. Russell had most of the ingredients I needed. I took a pail and went into the woods and picked salmonberries.

I followed Mary's instructions carefully, using her rolling pin and wearing her apron. To my surprise, I found that I enjoyed it. It wasn't nearly so hard as it looked. But I couldn't help feeling a pang for Mary. Here I was cooking for men to earn my keep, doing exactly what she had wanted to do. It made me feel unsettled in a way that was hard to define.

Mr. Russell was very cool to me all during supper that evening.

"I have a surprise, Mr. Russell," I said in a bright voice.

His whiskers jerked irritably. "I don't like surprises, gal," he said shortly.

But he would like this one, I was sure.

My pie was resting on a shelf under a piece of cloth. It looked perfect to my eye—but then again, so had the coffee and look what had happened there. Sudden anxiety flooded me. I took a deep breath and lifted up the pie, starting across the dirt floor. Without any warning my foot caught on something and I stumbled. The pie rocked in my hands.

Brandywine looked up sleepily from the floor.

"Blasted dog!" I hissed.

Father Joseph raised one bushy caterpillar eyebrow at my curse. I blushed but held my head high and carried the pie to the table. I put it down with a flourish.

"That looks wonderful, my dear," Mr. Swan said hesitantly. He turned to Mr. Russell and said, in a hearty voice that sounded forced, "Doesn't it look wonderful, Mr. Russell?"

Mr. Russell grunted, eyeing the pie skeptically.

I cut a slice for Mr. Russell and put it on his plate.

"Go on. She's been working at it all day," Jehu said.

Mr. Russell took a careful bite. Salmonberry filling smeared his whiskers. He chewed thoughtfully and gulped.

"Well?" I demanded.

The moment seemed to stretch out forever.

Mr. Russell didn't say a word. He just dug his fork into his pie and finished it in four neat bites. Then he leaned back, patted his belly, and belched.

Jehu roared with laughter.

"I guess he likes it, Jane!"

Mr. Russell grinned at me, and I didn't even mind the salmonberries in his teeth. "Yar good at pie, gal."

All the men clapped, and I flushed with pleasure. It was almost as satisfying as winning top marks for embroidery at Miss Hepplewhite's!

Father Joseph's eyes closed in delight as he took a bite. *"Délicieux!"*

"You should open a boardinghouse, my dear," Mr. Swan said, biting heartily into his slice. "You'd do a brisk business with all the hungry men out here."

"Just hire someone else to make the coffee," Jehu suggested with a wink.

When I went to bed that night, the aroma of pie filled the cabin. I fell asleep thinking of all the pies I would make William.

"My dearest Jane," William would say, smiling at me fondly, "makes the most delicious pies in all the world."

I was awakened by a small, soft sound. The sound of a fork scraping a tin plate.

The walls of the cabin were golden with dancing firelight, and the men's snores rose in a comforting way. It was an altogether cozy picture, which left me completely unprepared for the vision in front of me.

A strange woman was sitting at the sawbuck table, eating a piece of my pie, her back to me. Her hair hung in wet clumps down her back.

I wanted to call out, but I was too frightened to speak. Had she just wandered in while we were sleeping? But I thought Mr. Swan had said there weren't any other pioneer women here on Shoalwater Bay.

I quietly slipped out of the bunk. The woman didn't look up. She just kept eating the pie.

I walked closer to the table. Water pooled at her feet, and

the smell of saltwater steamed off her back.

"Excuse me," I said.

She paused and turned slowly, deliberately.

I stumbled back in horror.

Mary's face was white, her eyes black and filled with reproach.

She got up and walked through the door, disappearing into the inky night.

CHAPTER TEN
or,
A Well-Ordered Home

The balmy winds of June warmed my spirits. It rained less, and there was a feeling of hope in the air. Shoalwater Bay was an entirely different place when the sun came out, and on beautiful days I could almost understand Mr. Swan's fascination for this raw country, the way the mountains rose high and seemed to go on forever and ever, the blue sky arched behind them like a bonnet.

I counted the days that Yelloh had been gone, mended clothes, and tried out Mary's receipts on the men with varying success. Father Joseph built a small chapel at the edge of Toke's village, between the lodges and the stream where the Indians went to fetch their water. He was forever encouraging the men to attend his masses, and I considered myself lucky that I was not Catholic.

Mr. Swan took me on long rambles, pointing out local flowers and teaching me bits of the Jargon. It reminded me of going with Papa on his rounds when I was a small girl. My hand itched to write him, but I was determined to hold fast.

I walked on the beach and collected shells. Sometimes I thought I saw Mary there, her dark gaze fixed on the horizon, staring out at the wide bay as if searching for something.

But when I called her name, she disappeared.

"I'm leaving," Jehu said, slinging his pack on his shoulder.

It was a bright day, and the light made his black hair shine like a raven's wing.

"What?" I asked, startled. I was sitting on the rickety porch darning a particularly grim pair of socks that I rather suspected belonged to Champ.

He looked into the countryside, scanning the trees. "The *Lady Luck*'s all fitted up, and the captain's got himself some Indians cutting down timber on a claim up the bay. I have to load the timber up on the ship. Don't know how long it will take."

He stared at me as if he wanted to say something. It seemed so abrupt, his leaving like this.

"Well, good-bye, then," I said finally, swallowing hard.

"Jane," Jehu said. His blue eyes pierced mine. "If you need anything, anything at all, send word."

I looked down awkwardly. "If you happen to come across William, will you tell him I am here?"

His mouth seemed to tighten, but he nodded. And then he went away.

That evening at supper Mr. Swan announced that he, too, was leaving.

"Not leaving," he amended. "Moving."

"Moving? But where?" I asked.

He smiled in his jolly way and said, "Inland from the bay. I have fitted up an old Chinook lodge on a river up a ways."

"May I come, too?" I asked quickly, casting a sidelong glance at Mr. Russell.

Mr. Russell grunted.

The mountain man and I had struck an uneasy peace, but I was still uncomfortable living in a place where strange men came and went as they pleased. Mr. Russell let any passing pioneer stay at the cabin, and it was most disconcerting to wake up to a new set of unshaven faces each morning at breakfast. At least with Mr. Swan, I reasoned, I would only be living with one man instead of a whole gang. It was hardly a proper situation, but I was finding that one must lower one's good standards when on the frontier. If I was lucky, the fleas would remain behind in Mr. Russell's cabin.

"Of course, my dear," Mr. Swan said. "I'll take you round tomorrow."

We took Mr. Swan's canoe to the old Chinook lodge. It was one of several abandoned dwellings situated near the river.

The place was utterly desolate.

"Where are all the Indians?" I asked, looking around nervously.

Mr. Swan shrugged. "No one lives here. They think the place is haunted."

"Haunted?" I asked, and shivered despite myself. I thought of Mary. Really, a haunted Chinook lodge was the very last thing I needed.

"The Chinooks believe that their dead ones haunt the house where they died, and apparently a number of Indians died here. That one's ours," he said, pointing to a lodge with a chimney. "I built the chimney myself."

The lodge smelled stale and unused, but it was large, twice as large as Mr. Russell's cabin. Mr. Swan had divided the lodge into two areas and fitted up the sleeping portion with bunks. There were no ghosts in residence as far as I could tell. A thought occurred to me. Perhaps William and I could live here until we had a house of our own!

I recalled Miss Hepplewhite's words:

A well-ordered home is a miniature of heaven.

It was going to take a lot of work to make this lodge a miniature of heaven, I thought with some dismay.

But I did my best. I swept and aired out the lodge. I knocked down cobwebs and scrubbed the bunks with hot water to kill any vermin living in them. Mr. Swan transported my trunk to the lodge, and I spread a tablecloth on a table and arranged flowers in the crystal vase, which had miraculously survived the journey. I fitted two bunks with sheets and blankets, fashioned pillows out of linen and rags, and placed embroidered cushions on the hard chairs. Because the floors were hard-packed dirt, every footstep sent dust flying.

I recalled how clean and tidy the inside of Chief Toke's lodge was and the woven mats on the floors. Those mats would certainly keep the dust down. However, I was not looking forward to trading with Suis. Her success with my corset had not improved her demeanor at all. Whenever I went down to the stream to fetch water, I would invariably encounter her and other women. She'd say something I couldn't understand and everyone would laugh. It felt just like being back on Arch Street with Sally Biddle and Cora Fletcher. Not to mention, she was continually bringing me various useless handmade objects, expecting me to trade them for my last few precious belongings. When I would ignore her the way I used to ignore Sally Biddle, she would go storming off in a rage.

After a particularly windy day when every opening of the door stirred a cloud of dust, I relented and set off for Suis's lodge.

"Boston Jane," Suis said appraisingly.

"I need mats for the ground," I told her.

She had Dolly haul out a large pile of woven mats.

"What you have for trade?" Suis asked.

I had brought along a linen sheet as well as several pretty buttons. They were the only buttons I had managed to salvage from Burton the cow's rampage.

She took the buttons and sheet and eyed me suspiciously. Finally, she pointed to my head, tapping the bonnet.

"You want my bonnet, too?"

Suis nodded. The woman was out to get her hands on everything I owned.

"All right," I said, untying it and handing it to her. My hair tumbled down around my shoulders.

A group of nearby men paused in the game they were playing and stopped to stare at my hair. Suddenly Suis looked furious.

She grabbed my hands, and began to pull off the gloves, finger by finger. They weren't in very good condition, but still, they were the only pair of gloves I had left.

"What are you doing?" I said. "You can't have my gloves!"

"Gloves or no mats!" she hissed, her eyes flashing—just like Sally Biddle's.

I threw off my gloves, grabbed up the mats, and marched away, her triumphant laughter echoing behind me.

While I cleaned, Mr. Swan spent his days showing off the beautiful chimney. Indians from miles around came to admire it.

"Many *memelose tillicums*," Handsome Jim said, looking around the lodge, a worried expression on his face.

"*Boston tillicums* are not worried by *memelose tillicums*," Mr. Swan said.

Handsome Jim raised his eyebrows in surprise.

"Why not make fire pit in center of lodge?" he asked.

"Too smoky," Mr. Swan explained. "See, the chimney takes the smoke out of the lodge. This is how *Boston tillicums* make warm lodges."

Handsome Jim looked concerned. "But you need smoke for salmon."

Mr. Swan smiled expansively. "Ah, well, meat is kept outside in a smokehouse, built especially for that purpose. This also cuts down on the insects."

The Indians didn't look convinced and shook their heads, nosing around the chimney.

After one of these many visits, Mr. Swan came in for supper. I had prepared biscuits and gravy from one of Mary's receipts.

It had been a long, exhausting week. I had laid down the new mats, sewn simple curtains out of an old petticoat, and painted some pictures for the walls. It had taken me the better part of the afternoon to figure out how to rig up the curtains. It was a far cry from Walnut Street, but I was pleased with the results. No doubt Mr. Swan would compliment me on my skill and taste.

"That smells wonderful," Mr. Swan declared, pulling up a chair.

I smiled hopefully.

Instead of noticing my improvements, he started eating and chattering.

"Toke showed me the most interesting plant today," Mr. Swan said, taking out his notebook to show me his sketch.

I stared at him with dismay.

"It is apparently peculiar to the region, and Toke says it is very therapeutic for stomach complaints. Now, it looks rather similar to—"

"Mr. Swan!" I interrupted.

He seemed startled.

"Don't you like what I did?"

He blinked at me owlishly. He looked down at his plate.

"Oh yes, this is very tasty, my dear."

"Not the food!" I said in a frustrated voice. "The curtains!"

"The curtains?"

"Yes—the curtains!" I opened my arms wide. "And the bunks!

And the flowers! And the pictures! And everything! It took me *all* week! Not to mention I traded away my last pair of gloves in order to keep the blasted dust down!"

He peered around the lodge as if for the first time. "Of course, of course. Capital job, dear girl."

I felt tears prick at my eyes.

"I'm sorry, my dear," he said gently. "I'm afraid I'm not very good at these sorts of things."

I shook my head wordlessly. I had tried so hard. William was always so good at noticing. And then a horrible thought occurred to me. What if William had changed since coming out here? What if he had become like all the other men on the frontier?

Mr. Swan sighed, and we ate our supper in silence.

Despite Handsome Jim's dire warnings of *memelose tillicums*, I saw no ghosts. Nor did I see Mary. Perhaps I had left her back at Mr. Russell's lodge. But while we did not have ghosts, we quickly discovered that we had something just as worrisome.

A leaky roof.

"Oh dear," Mr. Swan said, peering up. "That does look bad."

It had been raining for the past several days, and I had spread the few pots and pans we had under the leaks, but the roof was clearly caving in. A sliver of gray sky was visible through the planks.

Mr. Swan scratched his head and said in a hesitant voice, "I suppose I ought to do something about it before it really starts raining."

The two of us went outside into the misty rain, and Mr.

Swan attempted to climb up to the roof. He managed to get one leg up, and the other swung wildly near my head.

"Perhaps if you . . . ," he called down awkwardly.

I pushed his other leg up and stood anxiously watching. After a few moments I heard bangs and an occasional curse. Mr. Swan did not strike me as a particularly handy man. Mr. Russell had taken care of minor repairs around the cabin.

"Drat!"

"Mr. Swan?" I called up. "Is everything all right?"

He poked his head over the side, his spectacles wobbling on the end of his nose. "Capital, dear girl."

A moment later there was a tremendous crash. I rushed into the lodge.

Mr. Swan was lying in a pile of planks on the floor, bleeding from a gash on his forearm, and there was now an enormous hole in the roof.

He groaned miserably.

"Why don't we ask Handsome Jim for help? It is a Chinook lodge, after all," I suggested gently as I went to retrieve some bandages from his gear.

"What a sensible idea, my dear," he said, sounding relieved.

Handsome Jim appeared bright and early the next morning.

"Boston Jane come help," he said, clutching new planks and pointing to the roof.

"I can't go up there," I said in dismay. Young ladies didn't go gallivanting on roofs, and furthermore, I had a terrific fear of heights. "Mr. Swan should still be able to assist you."

Handsome Jim rolled his eyes. "Swan too fat. He break roof."

I looked up warily at Handsome Jim. It was drizzling now, but I could tell from the dark horizon that a storm was in the offing. How dearly I wanted to be dry.

"Boston Jane, you not fall," he promised.

I thought it very likely that I would go tumbling, just as Mr. Swan had. All the same I scrambled up to the roof. I kept my eyes fixed firmly ahead and didn't look down, for if I had I'm certain I would have fainted.

"You don't faint at the sight of blood, Janey, so don't be fainting now," I heard Papa say.

Handsome Jim took the broken planks down and brought new planks up. I sat on the edge of the roof and slid them carefully into place as he instructed.

We bantered to pass the time. Miss Hepplewhite always said that young men and ladies should not be familiar with each other, but it seemed to me that out in the wilderness with no other ladies, the rules could be bent a little.

"Why you want Boston William for husband?" he asked.

"Well, he's very handsome," I began.

"Many men more handsome," he said with a broad smile, leaving little doubt as to whom he meant.

I could see his point. Mending the roof was hot work, and while I was damp and uncomfortable, Handsome Jim had stripped off his shirt to let the light rain cool him off. I must confess, his chest was a thing of glory.

Handsome Jim caught me looking at him and grinned teasingly. "More rich, too."

I shook my head at him, and we both laughed.

"Do you have a betrothed?" I asked, curious myself. There always seemed to be a girl trailing after him with moony eyes.

He looked at me quizzically.

"Someone you want for a wife," I clarified.

He grinned. "Many women want to be wife for me. But I not want to be husband."

"But you'd make such a good husband. And a modest one, too," I teased.

"What means modest?"

"Someone who is quiet about his beauty."

He raised his eyebrows in understanding. "Like Boston Jane."

"Ladies are supposed to be modest."

"Suis, she is not modest."

I thought of Suis's strange behavior toward me. "Handsome Jim, why doesn't Suis like me?" I asked.

"*Sick tumtum*," he said.

I laughed. "What? A bellyache?"

He shook his head and tried to explain. "Suis, she is most beautiful before. All men watch Suis. Now all men watch you."

"She's jealous?" I whispered finally, astonished. I didn't know which was more shocking—that the men thought I was beautiful or that Suis was jealous of me.

He shrugged and said simply, "*Sick tumtum*."

*   *   *

We worked steadily all afternoon, and by the end of the day the roof was mended.

Handsome Jim and I sat on the edge of the newly patched roof, feet swinging, admiring our work.

"Capital job, dear girl!" Mr. Swan called up.

I beamed. Who would have thought that I, Jane Peck, would have been able to help mend a Chinook roof? I felt that I could do anything!

By the time we had supper, it was so very late that Handsome Jim decided to spend the night. He refused to stay in the lodge on account of the *memelose tillicums* and bedded down outside under the stars.

The air had been oppressive all day with the threat of a coming storm, and we were tucked into our beds when the first fat drops began to fall. In short order the rain was pounding the roof like a drumbeat.

"It was indeed fortuitous that our Chinook friend mended the roof today," Mr. Swan said above the din of the rain.

"Yes, it was," I said, wondering how our Chinook friend was faring in the pouring rain.

Brandywine whined low as if he, too, was concerned. I had not wanted the flea-bitten beast in our new home, but Mr. Swan was very fond of him.

Moments later Handsome Jim appeared, soaking wet. He glared around the inside of the lodge, seeing danger everywhere.

"*Memelose,*" he muttered, but settled down next to Brandywine by Mr. Swan's grand fireplace.

The wind blew fiercely, and I was reminded of the terrible storm at sea, and of Mary. The world howled and roared all around the lodge. I wondered if William was out in this storm. Or Jehu for that matter.

All grew quiet and still. The firelight glittered, casting eerie shadows.

"I do believe the worst is over," Mr. Swan said in a hopeful sort of voice, peering around the room, his spectacles glinting oddly in the firelight.

And then all at once, a screeching howl rose and a gust of wind shook the lodge. It blew through the chimney with such force that sparks leaped into the room, and hot burning coals scattered everywhere.

"Handsome Jim! Brandywine!" Mr. Swan hollered in warning.

Both man and beast leaped out of the way, narrowly avoiding being burnt by the flying coals. The dry rush mats lining the floor burst into flames.

It was complete chaos. Handsome Jim and I were trying to stamp out the fires, and Brandywine was running in circles and howling and everything was confusion and then Mr. Swan hollered:

"Everyone be still!"

He shouted out orders: "Handsome Jim, put out those flames. Jane, mind the papers and maps! Brandywine, get out of the way!"

Handsome Jim looked at the chimney and said, "Chimney is no good."

"It is a fine chimney!" Mr. Swan insisted.

The wind was shaking the lodge, and all around trees crashed and fell with thunderous cracks.

"Chimney is no good!" Handsome Jim stomped his foot.

Mr. Swan glared at Handsome Jim. "The chimney is perfectly fine!"

At that moment the lodge shuddered and shook, as if some great giant was squeezing it like a plaything. Time seemed to stand still as Mr. Swan's beautiful chimney fell away from the lodge, pulling with it the newly mended roof and one of the walls in a tremendous clatter of stones and dust.

"Watch out!" I cried, pushing Mr. Swan out of the way.

"*Memelose!*" Handsome Jim screamed.

We stood in the middle of the wrecked lodge, the rain pelting our faces. The river roared in the distance.

Mr. Swan stood stunned for a moment, and then a look of pure panic crossed his face.

"The canoe!" he shouted, and tore out of what was left of the lodge. I raced after him into the storm, Handsome Jim right behind me.

We ran through the blinding rain down to the river where his beautiful gleaming canoe had been tied up. It was gone! It had been swept to the middle of the raging river and was caught on a snag. The powerful waters surged around the canoe, and it was plain to see that it would be swept away at any moment.

"My canoe," Mr. Swan moaned, distraught, crumpling to the ground, his face white.

If I could mend a roof, I could certainly rescue a canoe.

I ran past him and leaped into the raging river.

"Jane!" he cried. "No!"

But it was too late. I was in the middle of the river, the water up to my chest, the current rushing around me. It was frighteningly cold and my nightdress was heavy and sodden, the wet wool threatening to drag me beneath the surface. I looked around, squinting through the chilling rain, and saw the canoe at once. It wasn't far out, just a few feet really, and I waded out, struggling to move my legs through the mud and muck on the bottom. I grabbed at the slippery rope and pulled the canoe free from the snag.

"Boston Jane!" Handsome Jim called in alarm, stepping into the water.

"I do believe I have it!" I yelled over the rain.

Mr. Swan raised his fist jubilantly. "Capital, dear girl!"

Then the river swelled, sweeping the canoe downstream into the black night.

And me with it.

Papa always said you make your own luck, but this had nothing to do with luck. It had to do with foolishness.

Mine.

What had I been thinking to dive into this icy cold river? What madness had made me think that I could rescue a canoe? What would Papa say? What would William say? I didn't even want to think what Miss Hepplewhite would say.

I clung to the rope for dear life as the world washed by in a dark, wet blur, the river tugging at me greedily. I could no longer hear the sound of Brandywine's barking or Mr. Swan or Handsome Jim's concerned shouts; there was only the hum of water rushing in my ears and the crash of the canoe banging against stray rocks.

The river became rougher as the heavy canoe swept me down with terrible force and I clung desperately to the rope, the image of Mr. Swan's stricken face wavering before my eyes. I couldn't give up.

But with every tree I passed the current grew wilder, the rocks became sharper. And I was suddenly struck with a thought: I had never learned to swim. And where exactly did this river end? The ocean? A waterfall? Furthermore, I was a proper young lady. I knew how to pour tea and embroider handkerchiefs and paint watercolors, but I had no idea how to get this canoe back upriver, even if I did manage to survive. What if I died before William returned? These were things, I could see now, that I should have considered before jumping into the river.

I looked at the passing landscape and saw something—no, *someone*—standing on the bank of the river. I squinted through the pelting rain.

The figure seemed to turn to me, as if in recognition.

"Help me!" I shouted hoarsely.

And then I saw who it was.

Mary stood there in the rain, seaweed tangled in her hair, her skin glowing softly in the inky night. She held her hand out wordlessly.

I closed my eyes, not wanting to believe what I was seeing.

When I opened them, she was gone, and the river was carrying me away.

Who was going to save me? I thought wildly. Where were Mr. Swan and Handsome Jim?

Where is William? a little voice inside me cried.

Up ahead I saw a ledge jutting out from the side of the river and knew the sad truth.

No one was going to save me.

No one but myself.

In that moment I let go of the canoe and struck out for the ledge, reaching with all my might. It was wet and slick, and my fingers scrambled to find a handhold. For a brief moment I feared I would be swept away with the current but I held tight, digging my fingernails into the moss and dirt and pulling myself up with trembling arms.

I lay there on the ledge, gasping for breath, shaking cold and wet, and watched the river roar by.

By the time I made it back to the lodge, the sun was shining high in the clean blue sky and the storm seemed a distant memory.

I was wet, bruised, and extremely cross. I'd spent the night crouched on the ledge waiting for the waters to subside, shivering with cold. I had been so cold that I had resorted to burrowing under fir needles that had fallen from a tree hanging above. Now in addition to wearing a wet nightdress, I was covered with sticky needles. I'd very nearly died, and all for a blasted canoe!

I came up behind them.

Mr. Swan was sitting despondently in front of the demolished lodge surrounded by Chief Toke's family. They'd kindled a fire and draped a wool blanket around Mr. Swan's shoulders. Chief Toke was speaking in low, comforting tones to Mr. Swan, and Father Joseph sat at his other side, his head bowed in prayer.

The lodge was a wreck, the chimney tumbled over like a felled tree.

"My beautiful chimney!" Mr. Swan moaned sadly.

The Indians clucked sympathetically.

What about me? I thought. And sneezed.

"Boston Jane!" Handsome Jim exclaimed.

"Mon Dieu!" Father Joseph whispered.

Mr. Swan raised his head, relief clear on his face. "Oh thank the maker, dear girl! We thought you'd been washed out to sea."

Handsome Jim grabbed me and hugged me hard, patting me all over, as if trying to reassure himself that I was really there.

"Boston Jane, you not *memelose*?" he asked, his eyes bright with unshed tears. I was a considerable mess and had no doubt that I looked like the walking dead.

I smiled wearily at him.

"You strong, Boston Jane," Handsome Jim said, holding my hand tightly, gripping me like he thought I was going to disappear. Improper or not, I squeezed back.

"Or foolish," I said, pushing my muddy wet hair out of my eyes.

"Perhaps a little foolish," Mr. Swan conceded, standing before me. "But mostly brave."

"But your canoe," I faltered. "You loved it so."

Mr. Swan hugged me hard, and when he released me his eyes were watery.

"We can always build another canoe," he said huskily. "But we can never replace a girl like you, my dear."

Handsome Jim turned to Mr. Swan and hissed, "I tell you chimney is no good!"

CHAPTER ELEVEN
or,
The Particulars of Domestic Economy

That night we were back in Mr. Russell's flea-ridden cabin.

Mr. Russell just shook his head when he saw me and spat a wad of tobacco.

"So yar back?" he asked.

"It appears that I am," I said.

"Ya'll be fixin' supper then, eh?"

"I suppose I shall," I said with resignation.

Mr. Swan had lost almost everything in the storm except his precious diary. But he was most melancholy over the loss of his canoe. And in the days following the storm, he took to drinking liquor to console himself and spent his nights guzzling whiskey with whatever men were in Mr. Russell's cabin. I was reminded of the drunken men roaring on our doorstep on Walnut Street. Mr. Swan would soon have a cracked head like one of Papa's patients if he kept it up.

After a week of this nonsense, I woke him up early one

morning and dragged him down to the beach. I hoped the bracing morning air would sober him up.

"Jane," Mr. Swan moaned, his eyes bloodshot and bleary. "I won't be able to get my oysters in."

"Oysters?"

"Yes, the harvest is in a few weeks' time."

"I don't understand."

He stood and pointed to a shallow part of the bay. "There," he said, but all I saw was the bay glinting in the sunlight, the water rippling like a canvas sail.

"Those are rich oyster beds. Precious as gold. Men think nothing of paying a silver dollar for a shucked oyster," Mr. Swan said.

I knew that oysters were all the fashion in the States. Papa said there was nothing better this side of heaven than an oyster dipped in whiskey. Personally I found them revolting. They looked like dead slugs.

"Mine's over yonder," he said, pointing to an unremarkable patch of still water. "Toke helped me find it. But I can't harvest a single one without my canoe."

"Can't you buy one of Chief Toke's canoes?"

"It'll take ages to send word to my banker in San Francisco. And quite honestly, my dear, I'm fair broke."

I didn't know what shocked me more, the fact that Mr. Swan was broke or the fact that he'd revealed his plight to me. Miss Hepplewhite always said that matters of finance should never be discussed between gentlemen and ladies. Furthermore, if Mr.

Swan was in bad financial straits, how was his family in Boston surviving? Who was supporting them?

"I'm ruined, Jane," he said mournfully. "Ruined."

It had taken some time, but Handsome Jim discovered my trunk buried in the rubble of Mr. Swan's house. He dug it out from the mud and debris and dragged it back to Mr. Russell's cabin. I greatly feared the contents, like Mr. Swan's prospects, were ruined.

Sootie sat cross-legged at my feet. The little girl was terribly pleased that I had not been washed out to sea with Mr. Swan's canoe. Apparently my adventure was the most exciting thing that had happened since the British arrived on the Bay.

"Open the trunk, Boston Jane!" she said excitedly. Her English was, as Mr. Swan had said, excellent.

"Let's hope for the best," I told the little girl, and opened the chest.

Sootie peered in and clapped her hands.

"All is good!" she declared.

She was correct. It appeared that all was in good order.

I rummaged through what was left of my trousseau. There was one warm quilt, a stray pillowcase, several tablecloths, a number of embroidered pocket-handkerchiefs, underclothes, the Bible that had belonged to my mother with the family dates written on the inside front flap, and my etiquette book, *The Young Lady's Confidante*, which I couldn't help but think was utterly useless out here. I barely resembled a proper young lady myself. My entire wardrobe had been reduced to the Chinook skirt and calico blouse, and they were both in a very sad state. I desperately needed to obtain some fabric. Not to mention decent shoes. Handsome Jim had not been able to locate my shoes in the wreckage of the lodge. I could wear my wedding shoes in the meantime, but they were very delicate and would be quickly ruined in this muddy country.

I fingered the fine handkerchief with the embroidered violet and recalled the rush of pride I had felt at winning first place in embroidery at Miss Hepplewhite's.

Sootie grabbed the handkerchief and wrapped it around her clam doll like a dress. "Can I have this?" She smiled up at me with hopeful eyes.

"You *may* have it," I corrected her.

She squealed in delight and ran out of the tent, chattering to her doll.

I returned to my trunk and found my greatest surviving treasure, the one thing of value that hadn't been bartered away.

My wedding dress.

Next to it was the small packet of green silk ribbons William had given me so many years ago. I took one and idly started to braid it into my hair.

Sootie appeared in the door, dragging a very reluctant-looking Suis. She seemed strangely subdued. She had no doubt heard of my experience in the river with the canoe and wished I had drowned.

"Boston Jane good?" she asked in a tentative voice.

"I'm well, thank you," I said cautiously. Could it be that she felt bad that I had almost died?

Her eyes lingered on my ribbons.

"It's a ribbon. Would you like me to braid one into your hair?" I asked.

Suis stared at it for a moment and then nodded, her eyes softening.

I went behind her and brushed out her long, thick hair. She sat very still. It didn't take me long. When I'd finished, the ribbon looked like the first green spring shoot peeking out from dark, rich earth.

"Green suits you," I said, meaning it.

She touched her hair self-consciously, a little smile on her lips.

Mr. Russell had a scrabbly mirror on the wall. I brought it over to the table and held it in front of her.

"Look," I said, standing behind her to admire my handiwork. "You look beautiful." Her eyes met mine, and she nodded.

She looked curiously over at my open trunk.

"That's my trousseau," I said. "What's left of it."

"What means trousseau?"

"Things the woman brings to a marriage."

Suis nodded her head in understanding. "I bring three canoes to marriage. Slaves, too."

"You have three canoes?" I was suddenly excited.

"Good canoes. Father and brother, they make them," she said, examining herself in the mirror.

"Can you let Mr. Swan have one?" I asked. If Suis had a canoe, perhaps Mr. Swan could trade for one. Then his worries would be over!

Suis's eyes narrowed. "He have trade for canoe, Swan?"

"No . . . no," I said, my face falling.

"Maybe you have trade," Suis said slowly, looking significantly at my trunk.

I shrugged.

Sootie clapped her hands excitedly, and Suis began to hunt through what was left of my things. She tossed aside the books but pulled out the pocket-handkerchiefs and pillowcase, tracing her finger over the embroidery. She set them aside and pulled out a white linen tablecloth. She had a good eye. It was the best one.

"For the table," I explained. "To cover it."

Suis rummaged further. Now she ruffled through delicate lacy underclothes, pulling out a beribboned pair of drawers, turning them this way and that, inspecting them. She held them up to me.

"What for, this? Hold baby?"

I flushed at the very thought. Really, trying to communicate with Indians was very embarrassing on occasion.

"You wear them," I said, illustrating. "They're underdrawers. For wearing *under* your clothes."

"Like colset?"

"Exactly," I said quickly, anxious to be finished with this discussion.

Suis nodded briskly.

Her mouth dropped open at what she pulled out next.

"This like skin of elk high in mountain," she whispered, stroking it reverently. "This like snow."

"It's velvet."

"*Velvet*," she said, trying the word out on her tongue.

"It's my wedding dress," I said, wondering if I would ever get a chance to wear it.

"Wedding?"

"To get married in. To William," I said.

An expression of excitement flitted across Suis's face.

She clutched my dress to her chest. "I trade canoe for velvet."

"You want my wedding dress?" I was aghast. "But you can't—it's for my wedding!"

Suis shook her head as if this did not concern her.

"Do you know how much work it took Mary and me to make that?"

"Much work to make canoe! Who Mary?" she challenged.

"My friend, and she's dead!"

"Father dead," she countered. "Brother, too!"

I looked at the beautiful confection, white and creamy as a rose, fit for a real bride. If my prayers were answered, Yelloh should be on his way back, with William, but I had to survive in the meantime. I had no funds left and I badly needed things, especially some new shoes and sturdy fabric for dresses. Miss Hepplewhite's lesson on The Particulars of Domestic Economy (Chapter Fifteen) had been limited to advice on managing household money doled out by fathers or husbands. She had been rather remiss on the subject of actually *earning* it.

"Trade for canoe?" Suis demanded.

But how could I give up my wedding dress? The dress that had taken Mary and Mrs. Parker and me nearly two months to sew?

We had labored over every seam and stitch, endlessly discussed where to add each scallop of lace. It seemed that all my girlhood hopes and dreams were sewn up in that dress. To trade all that—for a canoe?

I looked at the growing pile of empty whiskey bottles in the corner and felt a sick sense of inevitability. Something had to be done about Mr. Swan before he pickled himself. If Mr. Swan had a canoe, he could harvest his oysters and lend me some money to tide me over until William arrived. And I grudgingly admitted to myself that I could make a new wedding dress, although it would never be half as beautiful as this one.

"Very well," I said in a resigned voice. "You may have it."

Suis looked down at the dress, smiling triumphantly. Then suddenly she looked up at me, a strange expression on her face, and fingered the ribbon in her hair. She petted the dress tenderly as if it were a kitten. After a long moment she put the wedding dress down and picked up the tablecloth.

"I trade canoe for table cover," Suis said, not meeting my eyes.

I looked at her, startled.

"The tablecloth?"

"Tablecloth," she said, her voice strident.

"But," I said, hesitantly. "But it's not worth a canoe. It's not a good trade, I—"

"Tablecloth good trade," she insisted, nodding. She smiled and pushed the wedding dress toward me. "Very best trade."

"Thank you," I whispered.

She nodded firmly. We looked at each other for a long, silent moment.

Then she snatched up the drawers with a giggle.

"Underdrawers, too?"

Mr. Swan was overcome when he discovered what my bartering had reaped.

"My dear girl," he cried, hugging me tight. "However did you manage it? It must have been a great sacrifice."

I thought of Suis's formidable reputation as a trader and simply smiled. "That's for me to know, Mr. Swan."

"In any event it was a very kind thing, and I shall repay you, I promise," he said, rubbing his watery eyes.

I nodded. It was very nice to see the old man smiling again. "Shall we go and see this canoe?"

Suis had arranged for Handsome Jim and some of the other young men to paddle the canoe to the beach. The canoe was truly something to behold. It was well over forty feet long and nearly six feet wide, considerably bigger than Mr. Swan's old canoe. Mr. Swan gave a low whistle of approval. "That is a capital canoe!"

"It certainly should hold one or two oysters," I conceded.

Brandywine barked at the men in the canoe, and they teased him by tossing bits of smoked salmon in his direction.

Mr. Swan grasped my hand. "Well, partner, welcome to the oyster business."

"Partner?"

I looked at him in astonishment. Respectable young ladies

did not work outside the home. It simply wasn't done. I couldn't go into business. Could I?

"But—"

Mr. Swan shook his head firmly and gave my hand a hard shake.

"I've got the beds and you've got the boat," he said with a broad smile. "We're in business! Now, what are you going to name your canoe?"

Brandywine barked loudly.

I smiled. "The *Brandywine*, of course."

Now that we had a canoe, we needed someone to transport the oysters to San Francisco.

"We'll get M'Carty to help us," Mr. Swan said.

M'Carty was a jovial fellow from Tennessee who had come to Shoalwater Bay around the same time as Mr. Russell. He lived farther up the bay and was one of the principal oystermen in the territory. He was responsible for purchasing the oysters of most of the pioneers and shipping them to San Francisco on the schooner he hired.

"I'll buy your portion of the oysters and pay you same day," M'Carty said.

"Capital, my good man," Mr. Swan said, rubbing his hands together.

"We have to time the harvest with the arrival of the schooner. If our timing's off, the cargo will spoil," M'Carty said.

"But how do we know when to harvest the oysters?" I asked.

M'Carty spit a wad of tobacco. He had the same disgusting habit as most of the men who congregated in Mr. Russell's cabin.

"Chief Toke will know when it's best to harvest. Seeing as we've got to use his men to help, we may as well go ask him."

"It's that simple?" I asked.

Mr. Swan grinned. "M'Carty is married to one of Toke's daughters and is a favorite of the chief."

"You're married to an Indian?" I asked. I must confess I was shocked. It was one thing to have acquaintances who were Indians, but to marry one!

M'Carty nodded. "That I am." He did not seem the least bit embarrassed. "Come over for supper sometime."

That evening M'Carty, Mr. Swan, and I went to see Chief Toke.

Suis greeted us with a gracious smile and we sat down at the fire in the center of the lodge. The tablecloth, I noticed, was lying across a bunk. Sootie ran over and hugged me around the legs.

Chief Toke was in very good humor. It soon became clear that he already had a bargain in mind for their services on the oyster beds.

"*Lumpechuck*," Chief Toke said.

"Blankets and molasses?" M'Carty countered.

Chief Toke shook his head. "*Lumpechuck*."

"What is *lumpechuck*?" I whispered to Mr. Swan.

Mr. Swan leaned over to me. "I'm afraid, my dear, that it is rum and water. Grog," he whispered. "The white men introduced it to the Indians, and while it is now illegal some of them haven't lost the taste for the spirit."

The Indians weren't the only ones, I wanted to say, but I held my tongue.

"*Lumpechuck*," Chief Toke repeated.

Suis sighed heavily. I thought of all the men in Philadelphia that Papa had treated and of Mr. Swan's latest trouble, and it seemed a shame that the pioneers had brought their bad habits to the Indians. Suis's eyes met mine across the fire, and I could tell she had the very same opinion.

M'Carty and Chief Toke argued back and forth for some time. Finally Suis suggested they gamble to settle the dispute. M'Carty agreed.

"They're going to gamble?" I asked. It hardly seemed a proper way to conduct business.

"Toke and M'Carty are great gamblers," Mr. Swan said, and he chuckled. "It's quite commonplace for people around here to settle disputes this way, my dear."

"What is the game?"

"They're going to play *la-hull*," Mr. Swan said. "It's a game of chance."

M'Carty and Chief Toke went at it with a vengeance, using discs with colored edges made from cedar. As they shuffled them around skillfully, Mr. Swan attempted to explain the complicated rules to me. In no time the lodge was filled to capacity with spectators, who cheered on the men with raucous shouts. The men's hands flew so quickly that I couldn't follow who was winning. It was hard not to be swept along in the excitement. It was a heady feeling, the notion that my future would be determined by a game of chance. But the whole oyster venture was one big gamble, was it not? As much of a gamble as a young pie-stained girl learning how to become a proper lady. It was, I realized abruptly, a gamble worth taking. Then a thought struck me like a rotten apple.

What would William say? Would he want his future wife working? How could I even consider such a thing?

I took a deep breath, considering the possibilities. I needed money. It was hardly proper, but if I had learned anything in this wilderness, it was that the rules must be bent on occasion. After all, I reasoned, if William had been here in the first place I would not be in such a predicament.

It grew late, and I fought to keep my eyes open. Smoke hung in the air from the pipes. And suddenly, I cannot say why, I was back in our parlor on Walnut Street and I smelled Mrs. Parker's cherry pie. I heard Papa's low voice reading "Rip Van Winkle." Oh, Papa—

"Time to go to bed, Janey," Papa said, his eyes smiling.

I blinked. Papa's face blurred, and before me was Mr. Swan, his hand on my shoulder, shaking me awake.

"Time to go home now, Jane," Mr. Swan said gently.

"Who won?" I asked, wiping the sleep out of my eyes.

Mr. Swan grinned jubilantly. "Our man."

The three of us walked back to Mr. Russell's cabin through the still, dark night.

"My father-in-law felt that we ought to wait several weeks before harvesting the oysters," M'Carty said.

I was still amazed that M'Carty had beat Chief Toke at a Chinook game.

"Why did Suis suggest that the men gamble? Chief Toke could have easily won," I said.

Mr. Swan cleared his throat. "I fear it was Toke who was out-foxed. Suis intended from the start to get provisions for her people, not liquor, and in order to do that she had to let her husband keep his dignity. You might say she *knew* M'Carty was the better player."

"You cheated?" I asked M'Carty.

"Not exactly. Let's just say my wife taught me some of the same tricks her father taught her," he said wryly.

"It worked out in the end for everyone," Mr. Swan said happily. "Suis got provisions, and we secured help."

At last—help for me to supervise! Although Miss Hepplewhite had given no hints on running an oyster business.

The next morning M'Carty sent word to the schooner *Hetty* to be in Shoalwater Bay on July fifteenth.

CHAPTER TWELVE
or,
The Great Mistake

The Fourth of July arrived with a cry and a shout, and also with every filthy, foulmouthed, buckskin-clad pioneer in the territory. Mr. Russell had spread the word that there was to be a huge celebration at the encampment and all were welcome, pioneer and Indian alike.

I'd been up since dawn laying out food, with Suis and Dolly lending a hand.

"Perhaps your William will show up," Mr. Swan said, rubbing his beard thoughtfully.

"Do you really think so?" I hadn't even considered that William might attend the celebration.

"Word of your salmonberry pies has spread through the territory." He winked. "Food is a great attraction to all men."

The day was hot and beautiful, and people started to arrive immediately. Mr. Russell and several other men had spent the week before the celebration constructing large, rough tables which had been set up in the clearing in front of the cabin. In no time at all, they were loaded with food brought by the pioneer men and Indians: smoked salmon, geese, boiled ham, bread, roast chicken, potatoes, salted fish, oyster pies, and, of course, barrels of whiskey. As the only young lady present, I received more proposals of marriage by more men in need of a good bath than I care to remember.

I was slicing a ham when I saw the unmistakable nose ring.

I could scarcely believe my eyes.

It was Yelloh. And he was eating a chicken leg.

"What are you doing here? Where is William?" I demanded.

He paused mid-bite, looking a little shamefaced.

"Mr. Swan!" I shouted.

Mr. Swan wandered over. "Is something wrong, my dear?"

"Would you please ask Yelloh here what he is doing eating a chicken leg when he is supposed to be looking for William?"

Yelloh spoke to Mr. Swan.

"It seems he came back for the party," Mr. Swan said, bemused.

"He came back for the—the—party?" What was the matter with this young man? Did he have no good sense?

"It is a great occasion every year, my dear."

Great occasion or not, I was exasperated. I grabbed the chicken leg from Yelloh's hand and waved it furiously at him.

"What about William?"

Mr. Swan turned to Yelloh and asked him a question.

"He says that William is now somewhere east of here, not far away from all accounts, and he will go and look for him tomorrow."

"Does he expect further payment?"

Swan translated, and Yelloh shook his head.

"Of course not. He'll honor your agreement." He paused. "And I do believe he told you it would take two months," Mr. Swan said, a gentle rebuke in his voice.

Still, he ought to be looking for William—not attending a party! I stared at Mr. Swan mutinously.

Mr. Swan smiled soothingly. "Really, you must have a little faith, my dear. He'll have your William back in no time at all. Don't worry. Yelloh is a man of his word."

I reluctantly handed back the chicken leg and looked hard at Yelloh, entirely disgusted.

"Word or not, if he doesn't return with William I believe I shall be driven to rip out his nose ring!" I shouted, and stormed off.

In their typical fashion, the men proceeded to drink every drop of liquor in sight.

By the time it was dark, they were quite rowdy. One clever fellow insisted on dragging everyone out to the cliff near the forest on the north part of the bay, where they constructed an immense bonfire. Mr. Swan was then called upon to give a speech. He stood on a rock, his plump belly outlined by the flickering light of the bonfire, and proclaimed in a booming voice, "Men of Shoalwater Bay, you are making history, forging a new destiny for our great nation!"

The men applauded with boisterous shouts, firing their rifles thunderously. I thought it most unlikely that anything but noise was being made—and certainly not history. No doubt every beast in all creation had fled the territory to escape the racket.

Someone broke out a fiddle and struck up a lively tune, and soon pioneer men were swinging Indian women about in wild dances. How I envied them! The sight of Yelloh eating that chicken leg had finished the holiday for me. Truly I had had enough of celebrating. No doubt William would never be found. I would be a spinster forever, as Sally Biddle had predicted.

"Enjoying the festivities, I see."

I looked up at the sound of a familiar voice. William?

"Expecting someone else?" Jehu asked, cradling a slice of pie. He took a bite. "Yours?"

I nodded. "You're back?"

"Got in today. Heard you've gone into business with the old man," he said. There were crumbs on his mouth, which he didn't bother to brush away, and I had to control my own impulse to reach up and wipe them off.

"Yes. Oysters."

"Good for you! You're full of surprises." His hair had grown in the month he'd been gone. Dark curls brushed the nape of his neck.

I felt suddenly unsure of myself and said in a rush, "It's just that I need to get fabric for new dresses and—"

"You don't have to explain to me." He rummaged in his sack. "This is for you."

He held out a bottle of New England rum.

"I don't drink," I said.

"It's not for drinking. It's for your hair, remember?"

"Oh." I took the bottle from him awkwardly.

The sound of the fiddle seemed to rise above the crowd, singing through the dark night. Brandywine howled and ran in tight circles, chasing his tail.

"Dog likes the fiddle," Jehu said, laughing. His warm laughter tickled along my spine.

"So it seems."

"It's a catchy tune. Want to dance?"

My stomach flipped in a way that felt very much like sea-sickness.

"Dance? I couldn't possibly." Respectable young ladies didn't dance at such wild gatherings . . . did they?

Jehu gave a hint of a smile. "Sure you could!" He grabbed my hand and pulled me toward the crowd.

"But but . . ."—my mind worked furiously—"but I'm not wearing proper dancing shoes!"

"You'll survive," he said, and I swear he sounded just like Papa.

Before I knew it, he had put his other hand about my waist—my waist!—and was whirling me about. The fiddle sang faster. Jehu was twirling me in circles, and the music was singing through me, the night air tangling in my hair, the world spinning spinning spinning, and I could not stop.

Jehu smiled at me, and his eyes were like blue sparks in the night.

He swung me around and around, and I felt a sudden rush of pleasure to be here, under this dark starry sky, dancing. How had I lived my entire life and never felt this dizzying feeling? It was as if I was being swept along, a canoe in the river, plunging headlong into the swift currents, not knowing where the next bend would take me.

"Having fun?" Jehu yelled.

Despite myself, I smiled.

He twirled me again, and as we danced I saw a woman across the crowd being swung about by a burly pioneer. Something about her looked familiar and I struggled to see her through the mass of people, but she kept disappearing in the crowd. And then suddenly she was right in front of me, her dark, grim eyes boring into mine.

Mary.

I stumbled.

"Easy there," Jehu said, catching me and pulling me up. "You all right?"

I looked up, but Mary was gone. A dark-eyed Indian woman was in her place.

"You look pale. Let's take a rest," Jehu said, pulling me from the crowd. His arm was warm and comforting.

He sat me down on a fallen log.

"What happened? You look like you've seen a ghost!"

I laughed shakily.

Father Joseph walked by and shook his head, his face a mask of disapproval. It was clear he had seen me dancing with Jehu.

I buried my face in my hands and groaned.

"Ignore the man, Jane," Jehu said.

"How can I? How can I when it's so obvious that he's right?"

"Right about what?"

"Look at me! Wearing this skirt. Going into business. And now this. Dancing! What is William going to think when he finally arrives?"

"If he doesn't love you, he's a fool," he said, his voice thick.

"But he thinks he's marrying a proper young lady and here I am behaving no better than a common trollop!"

Jehu grabbed me by the shoulders and shook me. "This is the frontier. Look around," he said urgently. "Just look!"

I took in the sight in a blink: men in various states of intoxication singing bawdy songs, pioneers swinging Indian women in wild dance steps, the flickering flames of the bonfire dancing against the inky night sky, painting the forest in a blazing glow.

"This isn't Philadelphia."

"But young ladies ought to be ladies no matter the circumstances," I protested weakly.

"There's no drawing rooms here, and no place for proper young ladies. But there's plenty of room for gals with grit and courage," Jehu said. He paused, as if taking my measure. "And you've got both."

I wanted to say that I had no use for courage and that the last thing I needed on this filthy frontier was grit, but instead I fell silent. Jehu seemed to sense my discomfort, and he looked away. He scratched absently at the scar on his cheek. My hand itched to touch it.

"What happened to your cheek?" I asked curiously.

Jehu shrugged, a bruised look in his eyes.

"Tell me," I persisted.

He looked down at his weathered hands. "I was supposed to be a farmer."

"You grew up on a farm?" Somehow this seemed impossible.

"Outside Boston. But ever since I can remember I've wanted to sail."

I nodded, remembering my girlhood dreams on my four-poster bed in Philadelphia.

"I'd dream of running away, getting off the farm, and becoming a sailor. We used to bring our harvest to the docks in the city, and I'd spend all afternoon watching the ships go in and out of the harbor. Sometimes I'd hang around the taverns and listen to the sailors tell stories."

"So you got the scar in a tavern brawl?" I thought of all those men on our front steps late at night shouting for my papa.

A fleeting look of pain and regret flashed across his face. "When I was fourteen, I made the mistake of telling my pa what I planned to do. I was the only son and expected to work the farm. Pa got so angry, he just picked up the nearest thing and swung it at me. Horse harness. Sliced me open. I ran away that night, signed on the first ship I could find. The surgeon stitched me up." He rubbed it, as if acknowledging that the surgeon had done a terrible job.

"I would have sewn it up perfectly. I won first prize for embroidery at Miss Hepplewhite's Young Ladies Academy," I said without thinking.

His eyes softened.

The wind shifted subtly, carrying a cool breeze. I was suddenly aware of the darkness pressing down on us. The night was soft as flannel. And all I wanted to do was pull it tight around us for one long moment and forget everything but Jehu. He sat so close I could feel the warmth radiating from him, smell his warm musky scent, of salt and the sea and something else, something that was only Jehu. I looked at his face, his blue eyes bright as the sea he loved.

"Jane," he whispered, and then he leaned forward . . . and kissed me! Me, Jane Peck!

I could hardly believe the wonder of it all. It was sweeter than Mrs. Parker's pie. It was belly-shaking laughter and heart-breaking sobs and breathless giggle fits all wrapped up in one long heartbeat that went on and on and on.

"Sweet Jane," he said.

All at once Miss Hepplewhite's words came back to me, like a splash of cold water:

Beware the Great Mistake.

"Oh no," I whispered, and pushed Jehu away. What was I doing? Kissing! And Jehu Scudder of all people! Good heavens! Respectable young ladies didn't go around kissing men, especially not sailors! What was happening to me? Had my good sense been washed out to sea with Mr. Swan's canoe?

"Jane?" Jehu asked in a startled voice.

But I was up and running as fast as I could on legs that felt like rubber. I scrambled through bracken and mud and muck. I had to get away, far away, from the terrible mess I'd made. I had ruined everything! Sally Biddle was right after all. Not only was I going to end up a spinster, but I was going to have draggled petticoats for the rest of my days!

"Jane, wait!" Jehu called, but I didn't listen. I just ran. In spite of the massive bonfire it was inky dark along the rocky point, and I could barely see a step in front of me. All I could think was that I had ruined everything, betrayed William, compromised all I'd struggled for with one kiss.

Beware the Great Mistake.

"Jane, watch out!"

Watch out for what? I wondered and then it was as if I had been pushed, my feet going out from under me, and I was tumbling, tumbling down a steep slope. I was tumbling through bushes and bracken, and I could hear the roar of the water echoing far below, but I couldn't stop, my arms didn't seem to work, and I heard Jehu shouting my name, fear in his voice, but I couldn't reassure him, I was too busy falling, faster and faster and there were rocks all around me, and dirt filled my mouth, and the rush of pounding waves, and all I could think was, *What bad luck.*

Then everything went black.

I awoke to the smell of fetid breath and something rough and wet licking my nose.

Brandywine.

"Blasted beast," I whispered weakly, pushing the furry face away. He whined.

My head was pounding, my mouth felt like wool, and my stomach was rumbling in a most distressing way.

"Aaah, you're awake. Thank the maker."

The room was horribly bright. I squinted but had trouble focusing on the figure, though I recognized the voice.

"Mr. Swan?"

"Yes, my dear."

I tried to sit up, but a pair of firm hands gently pushed me back. It was Suis. She smiled at me.

Mr. Swan came into view with Father Joseph peering anxiously over his shoulder. I could see Handsome Jim's worried brown eyes just beyond Father Joseph.

"Boston Jane, you awake?" Handsome Jim said.

"What happened?" I croaked.

Mr. Swan pushed his spectacles up his nose. "You've been out for almost two days. You took a capital tumble, my dear girl. Got a knot the size of an egg on your forehead. Suis used some of her poultice to fix you up. And the good Father has kept a vigil, encouraging all of us to pray for your recovery."

I gingerly reached up to touch my forehead and winced. It was swathed in bandages. Suis swatted my hand away.

"A tumble?"

Mr. Russell shouldered his way into the room. "Right over a cliff, ya useless gal!" he bellowed. His voice was as loud as a rifle, and my poor head ached at the sound.

"I feel terrible."

"Ya look terrible. What were ya thinking? Wandering around in the dark like that?" Mr. Russell scolded. "Ya scared us half to death. Poor Jehu is beside himself."

Jehu.

A moment later Jehu was at my side, and we were alone. For some unaccountable reason my heart thumped faster.

"Jane," he said. "How are you feeling?"

I closed my eyes, remembering the smell of him, so close.

Beware the Great Mistake.

Jehu took my hand and wrapped it inside his own. He stared at me with those blue eyes of his and for a moment I was almost lost, but then I remembered myself. And William.

"It was a mistake," I whispered, pulling away.

"Then it was the best mistake I ever made."

I shook my head, shaking away the memory of that kiss. I thought of Sally Biddle and Miss Hepplewhite and William, and stiffened my resolve. I had worked hard to become who I was, and I wasn't about to toss all that away because of one starry night. Because of a sailor with bright blue eyes.

He stared at me, a stony expression on his face.

"I'm already spoken for," I said. "I gave my word."

"To a man who couldn't be bothered to meet you," he countered sharply.

The truth of it infuriated me.

"You simply don't understand," I said between clenched teeth.

"I understand well enough, Miss Peck," he said bitterly. "I understand that you'd prefer some fool who has the good manners to abandon you on the frontier over someone like me. A scarred sailor."

"That's not it at all. It's just not proper—"

"The devil take proper!" Jehu shouted.

He turned and stomped to the door.

"You make your own luck out here, Miss Peck," Jehu said, and he was gone.

CHAPTER THIRTEEN
or,
A Valuable Rule

Another week went by, and it was time to harvest the oysters.

The *Hetty* had arrived right on schedule and was anchored in the bay, waiting for her precious cargo. I was sufficiently recovered from my tumble to take part in the activities, but the bruise on my forehead lingered, reminding me of Jehu Scudder. Jehu had not spoken to me since he visited me at Mr. Russell's.

We set out at dawn for the oyster beds. The sun shone brightly, warming our shoulders, and the bay was calm and smooth with hardly a ripple. It was low tide, and as Mr. Swan had predicted, hundreds of crusty-looking oysters were clearly visible below the water line.

"Look at them all," I said, amazed.

Mr. Swan had engaged Handsome Jim and several other Indians to assist us in the harvest. We used our hands and tongs and sturdy baskets to gather the oysters. When the baskets were full, they were emptied into the canoe. Halfway through the day,

I stopped to rest. I looked out at the water and marveled at the sight. Across the bay, the pioneers of the settlement and the Indians of Toke's village worked side by side gathering oysters into baskets. Mr. Swan was watching me.

"This is the best hope for the territory," he said.

"Well, I suppose the oysters ought to bring in some money."

"No," he said, waving at the canoes stretched across the water. "Indians and pioneers toiling together peacefully. This is the true bounty."

Mr. Swan had many peculiar notions. But it seemed to me that he might be correct in this instance.

By the time the horizon started to turn a kaleidoscope of red, our canoe was overflowing with oysters. I felt a rush of pride at the sight of all our hard work. I, Jane Peck, had helped in a real oyster harvest!

"A good day, my dear," Mr. Swan said cheerfully.

We paddled our precious cargo to where the *Hetty* was anchored, and I was startled to hear Jehu's voice ring out. I looked up and saw him striding back and forth, getting all the pioneers' oysters stowed away and ordering the men about so that they could leave in good time.

"Mr. Swan, what is Jehu doing up there?"

Mr. Swan gave me a considering look. "He's been hired on to captain the *Hetty* back to San Francisco. Their captain died on the journey here."

"But what about the *Lady Luck*?"

"Captain Johnson is taking the *Lady* over to San Francisco to sell the timber he's cleared from his claim."

So Jehu was leaving. I felt so many different things. It seemed cruel to allow him to think that I had any choice in the matter. I had made my choice long ago, and there was no changing it now. William was my betrothed. And Jehu wasn't. It was really quite simple.

I had to make him understand that it had nothing to do with him. I knew I couldn't let him leave without saying something. What I would say, however, was a mystery.

"Jehu?" I called from the canoe, but he just ignored me.

"Swan, get your oysters up here or we'll leave without you," he called. "We're making the tide."

"Mr. Swan," I said. "I would like to speak to Jehu. Can you help me up to the deck?"

Mr. Swan looked at me, a flicker of understanding in his eyes. "Of course, my dear."

Once on board, my courage fled, and all I could remember was a black starry night and blue eyes shining down at me. I shook myself. I had to speak to him. I steadied my resolve and walked decisively up to Jehu and then halted a step behind his turned back.

"Jehu," I said nervously.

Jehu whirled around, and his face darkened at the sight of me.

"That's Captain Scudder to you," he said coldly. The scar on his cheek twitched.

"Jehu, please," I begged, remembering that night, that kiss. "What are you doing?"

"What does it look like I'm doing? I'm captaining this boat back to San Francisco and then I'm signing on to the next ship headed as far away as I can get, maybe even China."

I held up my hands to stop his rush of words.

"You must realize I was overwrought, and tired. I was not myself. I never meant to kiss you!"

"But you did, Jane," he said in a steady voice. "You did."

And oh, how I wanted to kiss him again.

"Don't you see? I am spoken for," I said, frustrated and torn. *I have no choice.*

"You do have a choice!" he shot back.

"I cannot break my word," I said softly.

Jehu rubbed a hand through his hair.

One of the crew shouted, "We're all fitted up, Captain!"

I placed my hand on Jehu's arm and felt it tense beneath my touch.

"Please—"

He cut me off. "Unless you fancy a trip to San Francisco you best get off this boat."

"When shall you return?"

"What does it matter to you, Miss Peck?" he challenged, his eyes clouding over. And with that, he turned and strode across the deck.

Back on the beach, I watched the *Hetty* sail across the smooth bay. She disappeared with the setting sun.

And Jehu Scudder with her.

Everybody, it seemed, was leaving.

I watched in dismay as Mr. Swan packed a small bag. He had just informed me that he and Mr. Russell and Chief Toke were going to Astoria, a large trading post on the other side of the Columbia River, in Oregon. While I was not displeased to see Mr. Russell leave, I was less happy about Mr. Swan's departure. Most of the assorted men had cleared out since the oyster harvest, and I would be all alone in the encampment.

"Mr. Russell needs supplies and Toke and I have some business to attend to," Mr. Swan said reasonably.

"But who will protect me?"

"Father Joseph will be just down the stream at his chapel."

That was hardly reassuring.

"But why can't I go with you?" I asked desperately.

"You may come with us, of course, but what if William returns when we are gone? He is due any day now, I believe."

William.

Of course, he was right. I couldn't leave.

"Why don't you ask Handsome Jim to stay with you?" Mr. Swan suggested.

"How long will you be gone?" I asked, twisting my hands.

"Two weeks, maybe a little longer."

"Yar in charge, gal," Mr. Russell said with a warning glance. He scratched his head, and I swear I saw a flea jump. "Don't be giving away anything on credit now, ya hear?"

There was no help for it. I gave in to my fate.

"Well, Mr. Swan, seeing as you'll be in civilization, could you purchase me some fabric? And some thread and a new pair of shoes?"

"I can't promise the shoes, but I most certainly can get you fabric."

"Come on, Swan," Mr. Russell said.

I knew by the way he was pursing his lips that he was going to spit, and I quickly stepped to the side. Sure enough, a great gob of tobacco landed on the sand. But not on me! It seemed I had the mountain man figured out at last.

"Good-bye, my dear. I'm sure you'll be fine. See you in a few weeks!" Mr. Swan called happily as he walked down to the waiting canoe.

I couldn't help but wonder if this was how he had left his wife and children in Boston.

I stared at the empty cabin.

Since I was stuck, I decided I might as well take the opportunity to rid Mr. Russell's cabin of bugs and give it a proper cleaning. As Mr. Swan had suggested, I asked Handsome Jim to come and stay with me, and he readily agreed.

Handsome Jim helped me haul out all the blankets. I washed them in the stream and hung them on the line to dry, far away from Mr. Russell's cow. Then I dusted all the shelves and organized the provisions. After that I ripped off the horrible animal skin window coverings and stitched some plain curtains out of several embroidered handkerchiefs that still remained in my trunk. I swept every inch of the cabin and made Handsome Jim take down the immense rotten cougar skin and stow the stinking thing behind the cabin. I was determined to be rid of the fleas once and for all.

Finally I dragged Brandywine over to the stream and proceeded to give him a bath. He whined pitifully.

"You are infested with fleas, Brandywine," I said, scrubbing the dog's hide. The fleas fairly leaped off Brandywine and onto me as if trying to avoid their fate.

Brandywine jumped and splashed and attempted to run away, but I chased after him and dragged him back to the water, soaking myself in the bargain.

"Boston Jane like baths," a voice said.

It was Suis, and she had a basket in her arm. I expected she wanted to trade.

I let go of Brandywine and he took off into the brush, no doubt to find more fleas. I climbed out of the stream, pushing the wet hair out of my face.

"For Boston Jane," Suis said, and passed me the basket. "For lodge."

"Trade?"

She pressed the basket into my arms. "Gift."

I peered in. Smoked salmon and berries were nestled in the sturdy beargrass basket. The basket had an intricate design of a crane woven into it. I wondered how many hours of work it had taken to make such a lovely thing.

"Oh Suis. Thank you," I said. "Won't you come in and have some coffee?"

Her eyes brightened. Suis was very fond of coffee, although Mr. Russell had warned her to avoid any I made.

She smiled and sat down at the sawbuck table, and I put water on to boil.

"Do you do all the trading for your family?" I asked to make conversation.

"Women make best traders," she said, eyes flashing.

"Doesn't Chief Toke mind?"

She shrugged. "Toke gets what Toke wants."

It seemed so unladylike. I knew instinctively that Miss Hepplewhite would not have approved. "Boston women don't trade."

"Boston women, what do they do?"

"Do?" This sounded suspiciously like something Jehu would ask.

"I do many things. Trade. Fish. Paddle own canoe." Suis ticked off her list as efficiently as Miss Hepplewhite.

"Boston women are supposed to be pious and meek and modest," I explained. All at once I remembered Papa asking if I was going to let my brain rot and tongue drop out from lack of good use.

"What means pious?"

"To attend church. You know, Father Joseph's house," I said, gesturing in the general direction of his chapel.

"Boston Jane, you not go to *leplate* house." The Chinooks called Father Joseph "*leplate*" after the French word for priest, *le prêtre*.

Well, she had a point, but I had my reasons. I tried to explain in a way she would understand. "Pious means believing in the spirit world."

"You not believe in *memelose tillicums*."

I sighed in frustration.

There was a moment of silence and then Suis asked, "What means modest?"

"To be quiet."

She laughed and shook her head sharply. "You not quiet. Boston Jane, you not good Boston woman."

"Of course I am!" I clearly just needed to practice Listening Well.

Suis raised an eyebrow. "Boston women mend roof?"

"Well, not as a general rule."

"Boston women have oyster beds?"

I stared at her steadily, drumming my fingers on the table. "I suppose not."

She nodded her head as if to say, *Exactly.* "Boston Jane not good Boston woman."

Was Suis right? Was I no longer a respectable young lady?

I remembered Miss Hepplewhite's parting words of advice:

"Jane, you are entering a time of great danger and temptation. Remember this valuable rule. *Never forget who you are.* It is your duty to be ever a proper young lady and serve as an example that will make me, and your schoolmates, proud."

I fell into an uneasy sleep that night.

I was back in Philadelphia and dressed in my Chinook skirt, my hair hanging loose down my back. Familiar sights met my eyes—carriages clattering down cobblestone streets, ladies and gentlemen strolling, newsboys shouting.

And then I saw Sally Biddle walking down Arch Street toward me wearing my white velvet wedding dress, a man on her arm, his face bowed.

"Why look," she said. "It's Jane Peck, back from the frontier!"

Strangers stopped and stared at me.

"And she's brought the latest fashions!"

I shrank away.

"That is, if you want to go about looking like a filthy savage!" Sally Biddle burst out in peals of laughter.

The man at her side looked up, and I could suddenly see his face clearly. The gray eyes and beautiful teeth.

William!

I woke with a start. The cabin was quiet, save for the sound of the fire crackling and Handsome Jim's light snores. I groaned and pulled the pillow over my head.

I was just about to drift off to sleep when I felt the weight of someone sitting gently on the bed beside me. An owl hooted outside the cabin.

"Get off the bed, Brandywine," I muttered crankily from under the pillow. But the weight did not move. I held my breath. And then I heard the unmistakable sound of water dripping on the floor beside my bed.

Except it wasn't raining.

Slowly I peeked out from under the pillow.

Mary was sitting on the edge of my bunk, dripping wet, her skin glowing a sickly, unnatural white in the moonlight pooling through the windows. Reproach glittered in her eyes. Reproach and something else, something like anger.

She leaned forward, and water from her hair fell on my arm in stinging drops.

"No!" I shouted, and then she was gone.

"Boston Jane?" Handsome Jim asked sleepily. He squinted at me from across the room. The sight of his familiar face calmed me somewhat.

"I had a bad dream," I whispered, staring across the bunk. "About Mary. My friend who died on the voyage here."

He nodded. This was something he understood.

"Memelose," he said.

"No, it's not a ghost," I said shakily. "It's just a bad dream."

Handsome Jim shook his head. *"Memelose* speak in dreams." He pointed at my forehead, where there was still a small scar from my recent fall. "Mary try to kill you and take you to spirit world."

"Nonsense," I said. "It was an accident. I tripped."

"Change name," he insisted. "Change name now or *memelose* find you."

I shook my head. "I can't do that. It's the only thing I have left that reminds me of who I am. I am Miss Jane Peck of Philadelphia and that is that."

"Change name now," he said stubbornly.

"If I change my name I shan't even know who I am anymore!"

He looked at me with liquid eyes.

"You know," he said simply.

Being haunted by an angry ghost was the very worst sort of bad luck. For in the days that followed, it seemed I caught glimpses of Mary everywhere.

I would come back from the outhouse in the middle of the

night and there she would be, lying on my bunk among my rumpled blankets, staring at me with her black, angry eyes. Sometimes I would be awakened by Brandywine's soft growls to see her standing by the fire, her hands held out as if to warm them. And once I thought I felt her icy fingers tangle in my curls as I brushed my hair.

I took to inviting Suis and Sootie and even Father Joseph to supper as often as possible. I was grateful for the company and furthermore, I harbored a hope that the presence of so many people would keep Mary away.

One evening after a lovely salmon supper we sat in front of the warm fire. It had been a good day. I had not seen Mary once.

Brandywine circled the table, begging for salmon.

Father Joseph was instructing Sootie and Suis and Handsome Jim in the ways of the church. From what I had heard, he was not having very much success converting any of the Indians, but he was tireless.

He explained in detail how Jesus was crucified.

"Boston god is very bad," Handsome Jim said, narrowing his eyes.

Suis nodded in agreement.

"Why do you say that?" Father Joseph asked, perplexed.

"Boston god kill son," Handsome Jim said solemnly. "More bad than anything."

I stifled a laugh.

Father Joseph sighed. "I shall never be able to teach them."

Suddenly Brandywine started growling at the door. Someone

was outside, knocking. It was very late now and I wondered who it could be.

I went to the door.

Mary stood in the dark shadows, staring at me with grim eyes, seaweed hanging from her hair.

I squeezed my eyes shut, willing her to go away.

"Ma'am?"

It was Champ, the pioneer with the dreadful socks.

"Hello, ma'am," he said, tipping his filthy hat. His eyes were burning red holes in his head, and he was pale.

"I'm afraid that Mr. Russell has gone to Astoria."

"That sure smells good," Champ said meaningfully, sniffing the air. "I been traveling all day."

Traveling? Judging by the smell of whiskey on his breath, I thought it more likely that he had been drinking all day. Even so, I couldn't very well turn away a hungry soul.

I stepped aside. "Come in and I'll give you something to eat."

I sat him down at the table and dished out some salmon. He ate ravenously, as if he hadn't had food in weeks. When he had finished everything on his plate, I gave him a second helping. He demolished this as well and then leaned back and belched loudly. I had learned to take such belches as signs of appreciation.

"Thank you, ma'am," he said, wiping his filthy arm across his mouth. And then he sneezed, right across the table at us. I dearly wished these men knew the value of a pocket-handkerchief.

"You're welcome," I said, eyeing him warily, watching out for fleas.

"That was mighty tasty," he said, his red eyes lingering on Suis in a most ill-mannered way. "Yep, it surely was."

I was beginning to feel most uncomfortable when—will you believe it?—the man reached across the table, put his hand on Suis's bare leg, and grinned toothily at her!

Suis recoiled.

"Sir!" I shouted.

Handsome Jim sprang forward.

Sootie scrambled around the table into her mother's arms.

Champ acted as if nothing untoward had happened.

"It's mighty late. You reckon I could sleep here tonight? Russell always lets me sleep here when I'm passing through," he said. His eyes looked glazed and unnaturally bright.

"I think you should find other sleeping quarters," I said stiffly.

"Hoity-toity! All right then, ma'am. Should think you'd like better company than savages, you a lady and all. They ain't nought but stupid savages," he said, and spat at Handsome Jim's feet.

Handsome Jim stared at him stoically, but his eyes were challenging.

"You are not welcome to stay, sir." Sensing trouble, Father Joseph took a step forward and glowered at the man. Even though I knew he was a man of peace, his towering frame looked imposing. I could have hugged him.

"Stupid savages," Champ muttered. He got up slowly from the table and staggered out the door and into the dark night.

* * *

I knelt in front of the stream and splashed cold water in my face. Then I tipped the bucket and let the water rush in, wondering what to do.

A week and a half after the disturbing incident with Champ, Handsome Jim had awakened, burning with fever. I had bathed his forehead with cool water, but he had just thrown off his blankets and looked at me with fever-mad eyes, shouting, "*Memelose, memelose.*"

I had been nursing him for several days and now I wasn't feeling very well myself, although my feelings had nothing to do with Handsome Jim's mysterious illness. I had spent all of the previous night staying up with him. Toward dawn I had drifted off to sleep in a chair by the fire, only to be awakened by a cold, wet prickling on my spine.

A cold, wet, all-too-familiar prickling.

I'd opened my eyes to see Mary standing over me.

There was no doubt about it. I had to face the fact that I was being haunted.

How did one get rid of a ghost? There was nothing in *The Young Lady's Confidante*, I knew that much.

"Mademoiselle!" someone shouted.

I was so startled I dropped my bucket.

Father Joseph was stumbling up the path from the village, his face pale. "What's wrong?" I asked.

"The Indians," he said anxiously. "They're sick."

"What?"

"I'm afraid they have the smallpox, mademoiselle," he said, his voice breaking.

I felt the blood drain from my face. "Handsome Jim's sick. You don't think . . ." My voice trailed off in a whisper.

He nodded grimly.

"Oh blast," I whispered. "But who gave it to them? No one's been ill—"

I thought back to that night Champ had visited. He had seemed odd, but his behavior had been so atrocious I hadn't paid attention to his physical appearance. Suddenly I knew that he'd been sick. Had he known it? Had he known it and deliberately exposed himself to the Indians?

I felt the breath go out of me. "How many ill?"

"Three or four. The healthy ones have left, gone away. I've been trying to help, but . . ."

"Have you been vaccinated?" I asked, fingering the pox scar on my arm.

He nodded.

In the distance a bird shrieked.

"I greatly fear there will soon be no Indians for me to convert," Father Joseph said sadly.

The next morning Suis appeared at Mr. Russell's cabin with Sootie cradled in her arms. My heart went still at the sight of the pale little girl.

"Chinook *lametsin* no good," Suis said desperately. Sootie's eyes were closed, and her skin was hot to the touch. "Boston Jane, you help Sootie! Swan, he says you very good doctor."

"Me? But I'm not a doctor!"

"Swan, he says your father very big doctor in Boston," Suis insisted.

"But I don't know anything," I protested. "Nothing that would help her."

Suis held out her child to me, her own eyes shiny-bright with fever. Little bumps resembling fleabites had already begun to creep up her slender arms.

I hesitated. I was fond of Suis and Sootie, but what would happen if I tried to nurse them and they died?

A little voice inside me whispered, *Just like Mary.*

"Boston Jane, you help," Suis begged.

Boston Jane.

Miss Hepplewhite's words rang in my head.

Never forget who you are.

I was trapped, caught, between my past as Miss Jane Peck of Philadelphia and this other creature, Boston Jane of Shoalwater Bay.

What did one do in such a situation? There had been no lessons on this, no valuable rules about nursing dying Indians. There was nothing in *The Young Lady's Confidante* to help me. William would be here any day. My entire future was ahead of me. Wasn't it enough that I was already taking care of Handsome Jim? Wasn't I already putting myself at risk?

Papa's voice suddenly spoke loudly in my ear.

"It's dirty work helping sick people, Janey," Papa said. "But it's even dirtier work burying them."

I looked into Suis's almond eyes and held out my arms.

* * *

I put Suis on a bunk and Sootie on the bunk above her.

The remaining five bunks were soon occupied by other sick Indians who'd managed to drag themselves over to Mr. Russell's cabin and collapse on the rickety porch.

As the hours passed, it seemed that I cursed everyone. Champ for bringing the sickness, Mr. Swan for putting me in such a wretched situation, William Baldt for abandoning me in this wilderness. Even Jehu Scudder for not being here.

I tried to remember Papa's advice and did what I could to make them more comfortable. Father Joseph never left my side, and as much as the priest had vexed me in the past, I was grateful to see his black robes about the tiny cabin.

Suis was the worst. Little red bumps covered her skin and even her eyes. Father Joseph and I sat next to her bunk listening to her ragged breathing.

"God have mercy on her soul," he murmured, shaking his head.

The green ribbon I had given her was woven into her braid. The sight of it shook me.

"She is not going to die," I said firmly.

"Mademoiselle," Father Joseph said carefully, "she is very far gone already."

"No," I said, and I grabbed Suis's hand and clutched it hard. Her eyes were closed, her face flushed.

"Suis, you cannot give up," I begged. "Think of Sootie. And your husband." I swallowed, my voice wavering, the tears suddenly thick in my eyes. "And me," I whispered.

For a brief moment she seemed to turn toward me, but her eyes did not open. And then I felt her squeeze my hand softly, once.

*   *   *

Just before midnight, Suis slipped away quietly, without a word. In the end, her formidable trading skills had been no match against that greediest of traders—death.

I didn't think twice. I wiped her beautiful face and dressed her in my white velvet wedding dress. The soft fabric wrapped around the gentle curves of her body as if it had been made for her. She would be the most beautiful woman in all of heaven, of that I was sure.

Father Joseph sat with me while I sewed her body in a blanket. My hands shook with each stitch. The blanket would have to do until we could arrange a proper burial.

"Jane," he said finally, swallowing painfully. "I tried to help her. I swear I did."

"Of course you did," I said. We had both been running ourselves ragged trying to keep our patients comfortable.

"Not Suis," he said in a strained voice. "Mary."

I looked up from my sewing.

Father Joseph's anguished eyes met mine.

I knew I would never really know what happened that night in the cabin on the *Lady Luck*. But I also suddenly knew that for all his annoying qualities and his preaching, he wasn't a bad man. In his own way he was trying to be good. He was, in the end, another soul stranded in the wilderness, disappointed and far from home and everything familiar.

Just like me.

"I tried," he said brokenly.

I gripped his hand. "Dear Father Joseph, I know."

* * *

The next morning two young men died in quick succession. I ran out of blankets and had to use tablecloths. There were now three bodies behind the cabin.

We had just dragged the last body out of the cabin when Father Joseph swooned.

"*Rien que des sauvages. Pourquoi m'avez-vous donné aux sauvages? Je n'ai aucun espoir, je n'ai aucun espoir,*" he muttered over and over, babbling in French in his delirium. I touched his forehead. It was burning. I worried, remembering Papa's warning that the vaccination was not certain proof against the pox. I put him on one of the bunks of the recently dead.

I was on my own.

Hours passed. Then days.

I lost track of life.

Papa's words came to me often during that dark endless time as I brewed tea and changed sheets and bathed bodies burning with fever. His presence filled the whole cabin, and I could almost smell his pipe. I missed him so desperately.

"Sometimes all you can do is keep a person cool and comfortable, Janey," Papa said to me.

Handsome Jim seemed to be getting better and had brief moments of consciousness when he seemed almost himself. But Sootie was still very ill. She clung tenuously to life, drifting in and out of fever. I found myself bargaining with God for the little girl's survival. Let her live, I prayed. Let her live and I shall forgive You for taking Suis and Mary.

219

Was my bad luck killing all those I held dear?

I tucked Sootie's clam doll into her side and wondered.

It was dusk when Brandywine started barking. He was out behind the cabin, barking loud enough to wake all of creation.

"Brandywine?" I called, walking behind the cabin.

The dog was going crazy.

A mountain cougar was pawing at the dead bodies! It caught sight of me and snarled. Was it going to pounce? Brandywine barked wildly and charged bravely at the cat.

"Brandywine!"

In the end I didn't faint as Miss Hepplewhite had suggested. I ran back into the cabin and got Mr. Russell's rifle. I had never shot a rifle in my life, but I didn't stop to think. I just pointed it in the general direction of the cougar and pulled the trigger. The blast knocked me to the ground, but when I looked up the cougar was gone, disappeared into the dark, silky shadows of the forest.

Brandywine padded over to my side with a whimper, nuzzling his cold nose in my hand.

"Oh blast," I whispered, as I realized I had a fresh problem. The cougar had managed to tear the tablecloth off one of the bodies, and a brown hand hung limply.

There was no help for it. I had to bury the bodies.

The ground was soft, but in my exhausted state each shovel of dirt proved difficult. Very soon I could barely lift my arms. It was such numbing work. After digging the first two graves I

thought I should just get down into one myself. Why not? This was hell on earth, and it was probably my punishment for bringing Mary out here to die, for letting them bury her in her cold sea grave—

An owl hooted softly and I looked up, shaken by that clear sound.

The sun was rising, bathing the wilderness in a sea of pink light. Mist hung in the air.

And sitting on a log, wearing a dress blue as the sky after a summer rain shower, was Mary.

Except it wasn't the Mary who had been haunting me. Not the angry, begrudging ghost of a girl.

It was the Mary I remembered, the girl I'd known in Philadelphia, her skin shining, her hair gleaming, her eyes bright and full of life. Something thrummed in the air, a sweetness, that filled my heart.

"Mary?" I whispered, voice trembling.

She smiled at me, a glimmer of pride in her eyes. And then she got up, my girl Mary, and walked slowly into the rising mist. As her black curls disappeared into the dawn, I knew—I cannot say why—that I would not see her again.

At least not for a very long time.

CHAPTER FOURTEEN
or,
Thinking and Sewing

"*Come to the beach,* Boston Jane!" Sootie said excitedly.

Apparently a large whale had washed up on the beach. The little girl tugged on my hand and smiled up at me.

Sootie was much improved, and more often than not could be found at Mr. Russell's cabin, hanging on my skirts. She was a different child since her illness, quieter, and there was a lingering sadness about her. She asked often about Suis, about where she'd gone, but when I explained that Suis was in heaven she looked confused.

"Heaven is for *Boston tillicums,*" she said. "Not Chinook."

"Suis is with God in heaven with the angels," I said.

"God is for *Boston tillicums*. Suis is not with Boston God," she insisted.

I shook my head.

"What are angels?" Sootie demanded.

"Angels are people with wings."

Sootie regarded me skeptically. "Like owls?"

Father Joseph had survived his fever, but it was plain to see that he had done a very poor job converting the Indians, for they regarded most of what he'd told them as nonsense. In the end, Handsome Jim had taken the little girl aside and explained that Suis was in her canoe, and was now at the center of the earth, where she was most happy.

"Suis's *Tomanawos* is crane. When you hear crane call, *hooo-hooo*," he demonstrated, "it is your mother come to visit you."

Sootie seemed satisfied with this explanation. She remembered little of the horrible night her mother had died, and I was thankful to any god, Christian or Chinook, for that.

I was quietly thankful for other things, too. Dolly had disappeared, run away, in the days following Suis's death. While I grieved for Suis, I couldn't help but think that her death had given the young slave girl a new chance at life.

Handsome Jim was another story. His case of the pox had been mild, and unlike many of the survivors he had no scars.

No visible scars at least.

He had lost many close friends and something in him had changed. He was not the carefree young man he had been. He insisted that everyone call him by his new name. Keer-ukso. It meant crooked nose.

I was very worried about him.

"Boston Jane, come to the beach. Whale is very good," Sootie persisted, interrupting my thoughts. "Get Keer-ukso, too!"

"That's a fine idea, Sootie," I said.

We found Handsome Jim outside Toke's lodge. He was the only one there. Everyone else was at the beach with the whale. He was furiously carving at a piece of wood that I knew was going to be a canoe. He seemed to be pouring all his rage and grief into it.

"Come to the beach!" Sootie said, tugging his hand.

He shook his head grimly.

"Yes," I said gently. "Sootie wants you to come. You can't disappoint her."

Sootie smiled impishly at him.

Handsome Jim's face darkened, but he allowed himself to be bullied along to the beach.

We smelled it before we saw it, a pungent, fishy smell carried on the warm, humid August breeze. The Indians had already begun to strip off the meat and blubber, and the rib cage of the great beast was visible. Everyone was doing the greasy butchering work. Scavenger birds cried and shrieked in anticipation of their meal. Brandywine barked happily and charged at the gulls, scaring them off.

I was given a small knife to slice slabs of the meat and in no time at all I was as greasy as everyone else. A young man I did not know saw me standing there in my Chinook skirt, slathered in grease and blood, and said something that made Handsome Jim raise an eyebrow.

"What?" I demanded.

Handsome Jim's expression was serious. "He says you make good wife. He says he give you canoe if you be wife."

"Oh really? Just one canoe?"

Handsome Jim sniffed me. "But you smell like fish, not wife." And for the first time in weeks, the ghost of a smile flitted across his face.

"Fish, you say?" I demanded, in a mock-serious voice. I grabbed up a piece of blubber and threw it at him. It landed on his chest with a slimy slap and Handsome Jim went still, a stunned expression on his face. I froze, worried that I had gone too far.

And then he roared in laughter.

As a wave of relief washed over me, I remembered Sally Biddle and the ill-fated apple all those years ago.

At least my aim had improved.

And that was where I was, standing in the rib cage of the whale, when a party of men approached from down the beach. I squinted into the setting sun, the light bouncing off the glistening bay like sparks, and I could make out Mr. Swan, Mr. Russell, Chief Toke, and, farther in the distance, two other figures, one most definitely an Indian.

"Mr. Swan!" I called happily.

Mr. Swan waved enthusiastically. It was so good to see his jolly face.

"Good heavens, girl, you're in the belly of the beast now!" he laughed as the group drew near.

I wiped a blob of grease off my face.

"I daresay you had a boring time, then, without Mr. Russell and me around to liven things up?" Mr. Swan asked.

"I don't know about that."

"Didn't recognize ya, gal." Mr. Russell spat a wad of tobacco. It landed, naturally, next to my bare foot.

"It's a pleasure to see you again, too, Mr. Russell," I said with a sigh.

He snorted.

Mr. Swan passed me a sack. "I think you'll find these handy."

Inside was a pair of men's boots.

He shrugged. "It seems that ladies' shoes are not a popular item in these parts. Those are for a boy, but I think they will fit."

I looked down at my bare feet and wiggled my toes.

"You seem well enough, my dear," Mr. Swan said seriously. "I hear you are a great medicine woman now!"

"Suis died," I said softly, watching as Chief Toke caught up little Sootie in his arms and hugged her tight.

Mr. Swan looked grave. "I know. One of Toke's nephews found us and related the sad news. I'm afraid the old boy is quite devastated. She will be very much missed."

"Yes," I whispered.

"I'm sorry we were so long away. You see, we were waiting for someone." Suddenly he was all smiles. He waved a man forward.

Yelloh! The young man grinned at me, his nose ring blinking in the sun.

But before I could say anything a figure stepped out from behind Yelloh. I gasped.

I looked considerably different from the last time he'd seen me. I was wearing my Chinook skirt. My legs were bare for all the world to see. And I was slathered from top to tail in whale blood and guts. Even my red curls were smeared with grease. It's fair to say that Miss Hepplewhite would not have approved.

"William," I whispered.

"I'm—I'm—so happy to see you," I said, hardly believing he was standing here. His blond hair shone like golden wheat in the sunlight but he seemed, well, *smaller* than I remembered. Jehu would tower over him.

"And I you," he said somewhat stiffly, looking me up and down.

I hastily tugged down the hem of my skirt where it stuck to my bare legs. "My dresses were all eaten by Burton."

He looked at me blankly.

"Mr. Russell's cow," I explained quickly. I didn't know what to say about the whale guts. It seemed best to say nothing, judging from the expression on his face.

"I see," he said.

We stood there awkwardly. I was aware of the other men watching us with unabashed curiosity.

"Shall we go speak somewhere private?" I held out my arm.

After a moment that seemed to stretch out forever, he took it and led me down the beach, away from the others.

I hardly knew how to feel. I had dreamed of this moment for months, dreamed of a joyful, romantic reunion, of being swept into his strong arms. But now that he was here, part of me wanted to shout at him. The endless months of frustration poured out in a rush.

"William, what happened? Why didn't you wait for me? Our departure was delayed and I sent a letter and I know you never received it, but still—"

He pulled a crumpled letter out of his pocket. I recognized it at once! It was the letter I'd written him saying I'd been delayed. I looked at him expectantly. William shook his head.

"I just picked it up over in Astoria a few days ago." He looked out at the sparkling bay, the gulls crying and swooping low on the water. "I waited for you, Jane. But when you didn't arrive as scheduled, I thought you'd changed your mind."

I swallowed hard. It seemed a sensible explanation.

"But what is this about your negotiating a treaty with the Indians? William, what happened to your dreams of a timber business? What—"

"My, you've become very outspoken," he said, a gentle rebuke.

I swallowed hard, remembering my very first lesson at Miss Hepplewhite's: Listening Well (Chapter Five).

After a moment he cleared his throat and smiled at me formally. "But I *am* glad you didn't change your mind after all. It is good to see you."

I started to smile back.

"But," he continued, frowning. "This oyster venture of yours and Mr. Swan's."

I nodded.

"Now that I am here, of course, I shall assume responsibility of it. Such matters aren't proper for a respectable young wife to manage on her own, don't you agree? You have more important things with which to concern yourself." He looked pointedly at my Chinook skirt. "A new wardrobe, for instance."

Papa's voice suddenly thundered in my ear: "Janey, you're not going to turn into one of those useless women who care for nothing but dresses!"

I looked at William and swallowed hard.

"Then it's settled," William said, as if the discussion was over. "Now, regarding our nuptials."

The water lapped gently against the shoreline, and I had the strangest sensation of being watched. I looked around, but there wasn't a soul in sight.

"I believe it is best if we are wed at the end of the week," William said in a decisive voice.

It wasn't my imagination! Down the beach in the bramble bushes was an Indian girl, and she was watching us. A pretty young girl, shapely as a doe, with skin the color of cream. She saw me catch sight of her and ducked back behind the bush.

"Did you see that girl?" I asked.

"What girl?"

"The one in the bushes."

"There's no one there," he said. "Now, about the wedding—"

All at once I remembered.

"I have no wedding dress!"

"Mr. Swan brought back some fabric from Astoria. I'm sure you can make something up in time. I seem to recall that you are very skilled with a needle."

"Yes," I said, "I am." I looked at the hands resting on my lap.

They were hands that had harvested oysters, shot at a cougar, dug graves, ministered to the sick, and butchered a whale. Could these same hands sew a wedding dress? Would they remember?

"We'll marry in one week," William said in a firm voice.

One week felt very near, and my stomach fluttered nervously. Was it fluttering in anticipation or something else? But wasn't this what I'd wanted? Sally Biddle's mocking face danced before my eyes, and I forced myself to smile sweetly at William.

"It's decided then," William said in a smug voice, leaning over. "A kiss from my future wife?"

His nose loomed large before me. And for no reason I could fathom, I thought of Jehu's bright blue eyes. I pulled away with a jerk.

"N-no, thank you. We're not married yet."

His eyes narrowed slightly. "As you wish, Jane."

In the days following William's arrival, it seemed as if the strange Indian girl shadowed us everywhere we went.

"She is not Chinook," Handsome Jim said. "Makah, she is."

I was convinced the mysterious Makah girl was somehow connected with William. I wanted to ask Yelloh about her, but he had disappeared.

Handsome Jim also took to shadowing William. My friend didn't care for William and did not hesitate to let me know.

"Boston William, he no good," he insisted, shaking his head.

"He'll make a very fine husband," I said. "He's smart and handsome and—"

My friend put his hand to his chest. "He have weak *Tomanawos*."

I sighed.

Handsome Jim said firmly, "*Tomanawos* probably small mouse." He considered a moment. "Or flea."

"He doesn't have a *Tomanawos*; he's not Chinook," I said, exasperated.

Handsome Jim regarded me, a grave expression on his face. "You have *Tomanawos*, Boston Jane."

"If I have a *Tomanawos*, what is it?"

"Wolf."

"Wolf? That's not very good."

"Wolf is good *Tomanawos*," he countered.

"Why?"

Handsome Jim regarded me with keen eyes. "Most loyal."

In honor of William's presence I prepared a pie for supper. Salmonberries were no longer in season, so I used huckleberries.

"Delicious," William declared. "Better than Mrs. Parker's cherry pie!"

I blushed with pride.

After supper I sat in a corner and set to work on my wedding dress. Mr. Swan had brought back a bolt of blue fabric from Astoria. It was quite lovely, and I hoped William would not be disappointed that it wasn't green. In any event the blue was quite becoming.

The men sat around smoking pipes and discussing the Indian treaty. It seemed that William was very involved with the negotiations all over the territory. When I'd asked him earlier in the day why he was involved, he'd been rather evasive.

"Governor Stevens has been an invaluable source of counsel to me. I could not very well turn down his request," he said. "And it's a great honor, isn't it, Jane?"

"I suppose," I said. "But what about your plans to make your fortune in timber?"

"Jane, when would I have had time to start a business?" he asked irritably. "I have timber on my land. It will still be there when the negotiations are complete. And we must clear it when you and I begin work on our house."

"You mean you haven't even—" I was so upset I stumbled over my words.

"Jane," he cut me off coldly. "Enough questions."

Now as I sat and sewed I tried to untangle my feelings. I was very confused by William. Papa's words seemed to echo in my ears:

There are plenty of eligible young bachelors right here in Philadelphia. There's no call to follow one out west, especially one with no sense!

William's voice was getting louder. I looked up from my sewing.

"My point is that the area is crawling with Indians—on land that has been designated for homesteading. That is why the main provision of the treaty is to get all the tribes on a reservation," William said.

"Dang fool idea if I ever heard one," Mr. Russell said skeptically, shaking his head.

"Mr. Russell's right," Mr. Swan said. "Chief Toke will not be amenable to those terms."

"It is the policy. Putting the Indians on reservations is the only solution to the Indian Problem," William said firmly.

"Indian Problem?" Mr. Russell hooted and spat. "We couldn't manage without 'em."

"William," Mr. Swan said with a sigh. "There is no reason to round up the Indians. They're perfectly fine where they are. You know very well that we haven't had any problems with them. Why, you yourself have spent time in Toke's lodge!"

"Mr. Swan," William said abruptly. "I was naïve. I have traveled these last few months throughout the whole territory, and my eyes have been opened to the true state of affairs. You cannot trust the Indians. You have been lulled into a false sense of security by your isolation. Believe me, these Indians are unpredictable. Think of the Whitman party."

"Those missionaries were killed by Cayuse, not Chinooks," Mr. Swan countered.

"I've met men who were there. Women and children were slaughtered!" William said coldly.

Mr. Swan sighed heavily. "That was many years ago, dear boy, and I daresay there is more to that sad story than we shall ever know." He swiveled in his chair and looked at me for support. "Nonetheless. My dear, will you please tell your betrothed that he has the most incorrect notions about *our* Indians."

The silence in the small cabin roared in my ears. I looked at the bunks where I had nursed Handsome Jim and Suis and Sootie and the others.

"William, Mr. Swan is correct. Chief Toke's people are our neighbors and dear friends. Why, Handsome Jim—"

"This matter is of no concern to a lady," William interrupted in a stiff voice.

Mr. Russell chortled. "She ain't no lady. Our gal here has a mind of her own."

My face went hot. I didn't know which was worse—being told to shut up or being told I wasn't a lady.

I ran out of the cabin, humiliation coursing through my veins.

The next morning found me sitting on a log on the beach, sewing the hem of my wedding dress with angry fingers. I had to rip out the stitches three times before I got them right. I had spent a restless night in Chief Toke's lodge bundled next to Sootie and couldn't sew straight for Mr. Russell's words ringing in my ears:

She ain't no lady.

Was Mr. Russell right? Was I no longer a lady? And was that what was really bothering me? Or was it something else? Something that had to do with the way William kept dismissing me, as if my opinion were of no account. I thought and thought as my fingers stitched, trying to make sense of the muddle. Miss Hepplewhite's voice nagged at me:

Girls, you must strive always to please others and do so cheerfully. For this is where your true happiness lies.

Did my happiness lie in pleasing William and being the wife he wanted?

Suddenly Papa's voice spoke loudly in my ear:

Speak up, Janey. Say what's on your mind.

"There you are," William said, sitting down next to me on the log and sighing heavily.

I didn't look up.

"I'm terribly sorry if I upset you," he said, a contrite expression on his face.

Miss Hepplewhite always said that a lady should be gracious about accepting apologies.

"Apology accepted," I murmured, although perhaps not in the most gracious manner.

He smiled broadly. "I knew you were a sensible thing. Perhaps we should discuss our wedding ceremony."

"Certainly," I said, forcing a bright smile. Sensible thing?

"Now Jane, I was thinking that Father Joseph . . ."

But I wasn't listening to a word he said. For standing by the bushes, in plain view, was the Makah girl. She stood there as if she meant to be seen, and when my eyes met hers they returned my stare challengingly.

"That girl's been following us all week! Who is she?"

William clenched his jaw. "No one."

"William, I demand an answer." I wasn't going to back down this time, lady or not. "Obviously she knows *you,* because she's a stranger to me."

"She thinks she's my wife," William said evenly.

"Your wife?"

"Yes."

I felt faint.

"You have to understand, Jane, I thought you weren't coming. I thought you'd changed your mind," he said quickly.

"So you married someone else?" I managed to sound calm, but my mind was shouting. William was already married! Married!

He tried to put his arm around my waist, but I pulled away with a jerk.

"It doesn't change anything. It's not a real marriage in the eyes of God and church. She's just an Indian. I'll send her away."

I looked at him wordlessly. How long had he fooled me?

"Then why did you marry her?"

"The *land*, Jane," he said urgently. "I told you. When you didn't come I thought you'd changed your mind. I get to keep all six hundred and forty acres of my claim only if I'm married. I have to give back half—three hundred and twenty acres!—if I'm unmarried." He took a deep breath and plunged on. "Governor Stevens suggested I marry her."

I shook my head, speechless.

"It's complicated. Anyway, she's a half-breed. Her father was white. That's why I could marry her and legally keep the land."

"I see."

William shook his head. "I had no choice."

I flinched. They were the same exact words I had said to Jehu.

"You are the one I want, Jane," William said.

I knew that he meant it. I knew without a shred of doubt that he would put the girl aside for me. I thought of his clever letters, wooing me, playing on my girlish desires. Had he only ever intended to marry me to get his precious land? Had he changed or had I never seen his true character?

Papa had. Papa had known all along, and I had been too young and foolish and stubborn to listen. All those years I'd spent dreaming of William, dreaming of becoming his wife, flashed through my mind and all I could think was, *What bad luck.*

"She's just an Indian," he repeated. An edge had crept into his voice—or had it always been there? "She's nothing to me."

I thought of Suis and shook my head. Jehu was right.

I did have a choice.

"She may be an Indian," I said quietly. My throat was so tight I could barely speak. "But she's still your wife."

"My dear girl, I'm so sorry," Mr. Swan said.

I sat at the sawbuck table in Mr. Russell's cabin with my face in my hands. My cheeks were wet, my eyes puffy. I had been crying all morning. Poor Mr. Russell had been so discomfited by my tears that he had taken one look at me weeping in Mr. Swan's arms and fled the cabin as if being chased by a pack of wild dogs.

William and his wife had left, too. My future—no, *my life*—had left.

"What am I to do?" I asked. "I don't know if I can survive another voyage like the one it took me to get here."

Mr. Swan sat down opposite me and said earnestly, "You could stay."

"Stay here? In the middle of the wilderness?"

"Yes, Jane. Stay."

The word hung on the air, hummed in the still of the cabin.

"But there's nothing for me here."

Mr. Swan's face fell.

"I can't, Mr. Swan. You must understand. I don't belong here. I'm—I'm a lady."

A gleam entered Mr. Swan's eye. "A lady who has an oyster business?"

"Yes, but—"

"A lady who dives into a raging river for an old man's canoe?"

"But—"

"A lady who carves up a whale?"

"There are rules!" I said, exasperated.

"Jane, there are no rules here. And you *are* a lady, the finest in all Shoalwater Bay."

"What kind of future would I have here? You of all people must understand. Your wife and children, back in Boston . . ." My voice trailed off, but there was no mistaking my point. His own wife hadn't wanted to come to the wilderness.

Mr. Swan was silent and I knew I'd hurt his feelings.

"Papa said there are plenty of eligible young men in Philadelphia," I said in a small voice, realizing at once how very much I missed the sound of Papa's laughter. "And besides, I miss him. I miss Philadelphia. I miss Mrs. Parker and her cherry pie. I miss everything. I want to go home."

Mr. Swan nodded.

"Well, we'll miss *you*, my dear. You are like a daughter to me," he said heavily, his eyes watery.

"I'm sorry, Mr. Swan, but really, this is the most sensible decision. I must go."

The *Hetty* was due back in Shoalwater Bay in two weeks' time, and I would be on her.

*　*　*

It seemed no coincidence that the day of my departure dawned fair and bright.

A sweet September breeze was blowing across the water, much like the day we'd first sailed into Shoalwater Bay. The sun bounced off the smooth surface, and everything looked so beautiful and green that I almost believed that Shoalwater Bay was luring me to stay. But it was too late. I was packed and ready to go. I looked like a respectable young lady for the first time in months in the new blue dress I had stitched.

"Very well then, my dear," Mr. Swan said sadly.

Handsome Jim had refused to see me off.

"Boston Jane leave?" he said dully.

"I must. There's nothing to keep me here now that I'm not marrying William. I'm going back to Philadelphia and my family and friends there."

"No! Boston Jane not leave."

"But—"

His eyes were dark. "*We* your friends, Boston Jane!" he said. He stared at me angrily for a moment and then stormed off into the woods.

Mr. Swan and Mr. Russell carried my trunk down to the beach where I would wait for the *Hetty*.

Mr. Russell spat loudly.

Truly I was going to miss dodging his tobacco.

"There you go, Jane," Mr. Swan said, trying to put on a cheery face as he put down his end of the trunk with a small wheeze.

Brandywine was darting around the beach, chasing gulls, and Sootie sat on the trunk, like a queen on her throne. She didn't quite understand that I was leaving for good. She thought I was moving for the winter, the way her family left Shoalwater Bay in winter. I didn't try to correct her.

Mr. Russell took off his cap, scratching his head. Would the man ever be rid of fleas?

"Good luck, gal," Mr. Russell said. He seemed on the verge of saying something else, but then simply shook his head and turned and walked over the dunes.

Mr. Swan was trying to be jovial, but it was clear that he was still quite unhappy with my decision.

"Now you will be sure to keep in touch. We have business, you and I," he said, his throat catching.

"Yes, of course," I said stiffly.

He held out a bag. "A small present for your leave-taking. There is never anything decent to eat aboard a ship."

Small clusters of strange-looking fruit attached to branches rested inside the cloth.

"They're crab apples. Quite tart, but I've acquired a taste for them," he said with a forced smile. "Perhaps you can make one of your famous pies."

"Thank you," I said. "The food was certainly terrible on the voyage here."

He swallowed hard. "You'll forgive me if I don't see you off. I'm not very good at farewells," he said, and turned and strode away.

The previous day, Father Joseph had stopped by as I was packing, a packet of letters in his hand.

"For the bishop," he explained.

I nodded and took the packet.

He regarded me silently. I remembered the outbound voyage on the *Lady Luck* and everything that had happened since. Father Joseph was woven up in all my memories.

"I'll miss you, Father," I said, and hugged him impulsively.

Father Joseph swallowed, his eyebrows knitted in concern.

"God watch over you, *ma chère*," he said.

The *Hetty* sailed into the bay, its white sails fluttering. A sudden wind rose and blew over me, gentle as a kiss, the air smelling sweetly of salt and the sea.

Jehu.

I wondered if he still hated me, halfway to China.

Brandywine nuzzled his cold nose expectantly in my hand.

"I have no food, Brandywine," I said. "But I shall miss you."

Sootie was playing in a shallow tide pool, splashing about. I slipped off my new boots and joined her. The water was cool, the sand hard beneath my feet. She made a face at the water.

"Pretty Sootie!" she declared.

I studied my reflection in the water. The sunburned face, the round cheeks, the nose dotted with freckles, hair unbound and fluttering wildly in the wind. The girl looking back at me bore no resemblance to the thin, pale, quiet, tidy, proper creature that had departed Philadelphia so many months ago.

The *Hetty* dropped anchor, and a rowboat was being lowered.

I put on my boots, picked up my case, and stood patiently on the sand. I looked at the sack in my hand and pulled out one of the odd little crab apples.

And the strangest thing happened. Will you believe it?

It all came rushing back.

Being eleven years old and laughing with Jebediah Parker. The sun shining down as if it would shine forever. The feel of a rotten apple, heavy in my hand. How at that moment the future seemed full of possibility, the whole world stretched out like Mrs. Parker's cherry pie, just waiting for me to take a bite.

How I was the luckiest girl in the world.

"Jane!"

I looked up. Jehu was waving to me from the rowboat.

And he was smiling!

I stood on the beach, my heart thudding in my chest. My life felt as tangled and messy as my red hair. How had I gotten to this sorry state? I had been such a happy girl. Had my life truly been determined by the unlucky flight of a rotten apple?

Certainly not.

I was Miss Jane Peck of Philadelphia. I was also Boston Jane of Shoalwater Bay.

By any name, I had a choice.

I took a deep breath and smiled at Jehu.

Papa always said you make your own luck.

And maybe you do.

The End

AUTHOR'S NOTE

I was inspired to write *Boston Jane* after reading *Skulduggery on Shoalwater Bay*, a book of poetry by Willard Espy, about the nineteenth-century pioneers and Indians on Shoalwater Bay. One of the pioneers he wrote a poem about was James G. Swan.

James G. Swan, an enigmatic and self-proclaimed adventurer, abandoned a comfortable middle-class life and family in Boston to go and live on Shoalwater Bay (now known as Willapa Bay) in the Washington Territory in 1852. He wrote a fascinating account of his stay at Shoalwater Bay entitled *The Northwest Coast, Or, Three Years' Residence in Washington Territory* that was published in 1857 by Harper & Brothers.

James G. Swan was very interested in the Indians residing at Shoalwater Bay and spent much of his time learning their languages, sleeping in their lodges, and living and working alongside them. In fact, he went on a fishing trip with a group of Chinooks on the Naselle River, the setting of my first book, *Our Only May Amelia*.

The Chinooks residing at Shoalwater Bay spoke both the

Chinook language and the Chinook Jargon, a trade language that was used for generations by many Pacific Northwest tribes to communicate with each other and with the Europeans when they arrived. Both the pure Chinook and the Jargon were spoken languages, not written, and so different spellings exist in varying accounts.

In keeping with the spirit of James Swan, I have generally used his spellings in *Boston Jane*. Also, like Handsome Jim and Suis, some of the Indians spoke English fluently, the children generally more so. However, Swan took pains to point out in his book that many Chinook felt they already had a perfectly good, extremely flexible trade language in the Jargon, and therefore had no use for English. Thus quite a few Europeans made regular use of the Jargon, and several dictionaries of the Jargon exist.

James G. Swan was characteristic of the typical nineteenth-century white man in that he subscribed to many of the attitudes of his time and the prejudices that came along with them. However, in other respects he was a surprisingly open-minded and unbiased observer, who genuinely seemed to care about the Chinook way of life and their fate. These contradictions were what made him so interesting to me, and were why I couldn't resist writing about him. I think the James Swan in *Boston Jane* is a little romanticized compared to the real man, but I hope I'll be forgiven a bit of poetic license.

Although this is a work of fiction, I have incorporated several real-life incidents in *Boston Jane*, specifically Mr. Swan's ill-fated experience with the chimney and the canoe, the smallpox outbreak, and the Fourth of July celebration. The character I have tried to bring to life in this book was inspired by some of his own remarks, for example: "This is the best method of traveling in any Indian country; that is to say, always have some Indians in the company . . ." Swan never once hinted at why he was willing to leave his family alone in Boston for three years: this is perhaps the greatest mystery in *The Northwest Coast*, and I have entirely invented Mrs. Swan's motivations in this book.

I was so excited by my research that I named many of my characters after other historical residents of Shoalwater Bay, including Chief Toke, Suis, Mr. Russell, Father Joseph, Champ, M'Carty, Dolly, Jehu Scudder, and William Baldt. I have fictionalized these characters in all instances. In real life, Father Joseph Lionnet was actually a missionary at Chinook, Washington. By all accounts, the real Father Joseph was equally unsuccessful at convincing the Chinook that his ways were better than theirs.

Brandywine the dog was entirely made up, but bears a remarkable resemblance to a certain animal I know who is always begging for food. However, the *Brandywine* was a frigate that gave the real M'Carty his nickname, Old Brandywine.

Incidentally, conditions aboard brigs sailing around Cape Horn were often every bit as bad as I have described them. I ran across an account in which a paying passenger suffered so much that he actually jumped ship at Valparaiso and signed on as a working hand on another ship bound for San Francisco.

Finally, I based Miss Hepplewhite's teachings and Jane's etiquette book, *The Young Lady's Confidante*, on a popular nineteenth-century etiquette book, *The Young Lady's Friend* by Mrs. John Farrar. Mrs. Farrar was such a respectable lady, and writing a book was so unseemly for a woman of her times, that the first few editions of *The Young Lady's Friend* had only the words "By a Lady" on the cover. In some instances I have used the actual instruction from *The Young Lady's Friend* in Miss Hepplewhite's dialogue and in *The Young Lady's Confidante* (will you believe it!).

"There is more to be learned about pouring out tea and coffee, than most young ladies are willing to believe."

RESOURCES

Chinook Tribal Office, Chinook, Washington.

Pacific County Historical Society and Museum, South Bend, Washington.

The Northwest Coast, Or, Three Years' Residence in Washington Territory, James G. Swan, University of Washington Press.

Skulduggery on Shoalwater Bay, Willard R. Espy. Illustrated by Nancy Lloyd, Cranberry Press.

ABOUT THE AUTHOR

Jennifer L. Holm is the author of two Newbery Honor books, *Our Only May Amelia* and *Penny from Heaven*. She is also the author of several other highly praised books, including the Boston Jane trilogy, *Middle School Is Worse Than Meatloaf*, and the Babymouse series, which she collaborates on with her brother, Matthew Holm. Jennifer lives in California with her husband and their two children. You can visit her on the Web at www.jenniferholm.com.

Don't miss book 2
in the Boston Jane trilogy

Available from Yearling in May 2010!
Turn the page for a sneak peek.

CHAPTER ONE
or,
The Luckiest Girl

It was a sweet September day on the beach, much like the day I'd first sailed into Shoalwater Bay that April. The sun was skipping across the water, and the sky was a bright arc of blue racing to impossibly tall green trees. And for the first time since arriving on this wild stretch of wilderness, I felt lucky again.

You see, I had survived these many months in the company of rough men and Chinook Indians, not to mention a flea-ridden hound, and while it was true that my wardrobe had suffered greatly, one might say that my person had thrived. I had made friends. I had started an oyster business. I had survived endless calamity: six months of seasickness on the voyage from Philadelphia, a near-drowning, a fall from a cliff, and a smallpox outbreak. What was there to stop me now?

Although a life on the rugged frontier of the Washington Territory was not recommended for a proper young lady of sixteen, especially in the absence of a suitable chaperone, I intended to try it.

After all, I did make the best pies on Shoalwater Bay. And striding up the beach toward me was a man who appreciated them.

"Jane!"

He had the bluest eyes I had ever seen, bluer than the water of the bay behind him. A schooner, the *Hetty*, was anchored not far out, and it was the reason I had packed all my belongings and was standing beside my trunk. The same schooner had brought Jehu Scudder back to the bay after a prolonged absence. Indeed, when Jehu left, I had doubted that I would ever see him again.

"Jane," Jehu said gruffly, his thick black hair brushing his shoulders, his eyes glowing in his tanned face. I had last seen him nearly two months ago, at which time I had hurt his feelings, and sailor that he was, he had vowed to sail as far away as China to be rid of me.

"Jehu," I replied, nervously pushing a sticky tangle of red curls off my cheeks.

He shook his head. "You're looking well, Miss Peck."

"As are you, Mr. Scudder," I replied, my voice light.

We stood there for a moment just looking at each other, the soft bay air brushing between us like a ribbon. Without thinking, I took a step forward, toward him, until I was so close that I breathed the scent of the saltwater on his skin. And all at once I remembered that night, those stars, his cheek close to mine.

"Boston Jane! Boston Jane!" a small voice behind me cried.

Sootie, a Chinook girl who had become dear to me, came rushing down the beach, little legs pumping, her feet wet from the tide pool in which she had been playing. She was waving a particularly large clamshell at me, of the sort the Chinook children often fashioned into dolls.

"Look what I found!" she said, eyeing Jehu.

"Sootie," I said, smoothing back her thick black hair. "You remember Captain Scudder? He was the first mate on the *Lady Luck*, the ship that brought me here from Philadelphia."

Sootie clutched the skirts of my blue calico dress and hid behind them shyly, peeking out at Jehu with her bright brown eyes. Her mother, my friend Suis, had died in the summer smallpox outbreak, and since then Sootie had spent a great deal of time in my company.

Jehu crouched down next to her, admiring her find. "That's a real nice shell you have there."

She grinned flirtatiously at him, exposing a gap where one of her new front teeth was coming in.

Jehu grinned right back and squinted up at me from where he knelt. "I see you took my advice about wearing blue. Although I did like that Chinook skirt of yours," he teased, his Boston accent dry as a burr.

The cedar bark skirt in question, while very comfortable, had left my legs quite bare. "That skirt was hardly proper, Jehu," I rebuked him gently.

At this, his lips tightened and a shuttered look came across his face. The thick angry scar on his cheek twitched in a familiar way. He hunched his shoulders forward and stood up, deliberately looking somewhere over my shoulder. "Ah, yes, proper."

I bit my lip and stepped back. I had little doubt as to what was causing this sudden transformation. I had rejected his affections, as I had been engaged to another man.

"So tell me, how is your new husband?" he asked in a clipped voice.

"Jehu," I said quickly.

He turned from me and stared angrily out at the smooth bay. "If you'll excuse me, I've got supplies to deliver," he said tersely, and then he turned on his booted heel and strode quickly down the beach away from me.

I took a step forward, Sootie's arms tight around my legs. What was I to do? Miss Hepplewhite, my instructor at the Young Ladies Academy in Philadelphia, had a great number of opinions on the proper behavior of a young lady. I had discovered, however, that many of her careful instructions were sorely lacking when it came to surviving on the frontier. There was not much call for pouring tea or embroidering handkerchiefs in the wilds of Shoalwater Bay. And I certainly didn't recall any helpful hints on how to prevent the only man one had ever kissed from storming away for the second time in one's life. So I did something that I was sure would have shocked my old teacher.

I shouted.

"I didn't marry him!"

He froze and then turned back toward me, walking fast. He grabbed my shoulders and looked down into my eyes.

"You didn't?" Something indefinable flickered across his face.

"It seems that Mr. Baldt already had a wife."

Jehu slapped his thigh triumphantly. "I knew he was no good!"

The difficulties of this year, 1854, had culminated in the sad discovery that the man I had sailed around two continents to marry, William Baldt, had married another before I could arrive. Papa would not have been surprised. Like Jehu, he had a very poor opinion of William Baldt.

"Janey," my white-bearded papa had told me firmly when I declared my intention to accept Mr. Baldt's proposal, "you are transfixed with William for the wrong reasons. There's nothing for you out on that frontier. It's dangerous. There are plenty of eligible young bachelors right here in Philadelphia. There's no call to follow one out west, especially one with no sense."

I confess that I couldn't help but wonder what Papa would think of Jehu. My sweet surgeon father had always been fond of sailors. Why, they were generally his best clients, considering the number of cracked heads that required stitching from drunken bar brawls.

"You're leaving then?" Jehu asked quietly, gesturing to my trunk on the beach.

That morning upon waking I'd had every intention of leaving Shoalwater Bay and all of its inhabitants behind me. After my engagement to William Baldt had fallen apart two weeks earlier, I had arranged for passage back to San Francisco on the schooner *Hetty*, which was due to arrive with supplies. I had bidden my farewells and taken my trunk down to the beach that morning fully expecting to depart the shores of the bay forever.

But as I had watched the *Hetty* sail in, and considered all I had been through—and survived—I had realized that I could follow my sweet papa's advice, and make my own luck right here in Shoalwater Bay.

"Are you going away, Boston Jane?" Sootie asked anxiously, clutching me fiercely around the legs, as if by force alone she could prevent my departure.

Speak up, Janey. Say what's on your mind, Papa always said.

I looked into Jehu's clear eyes, and said to Sootie, my voice shaking slightly, "No. I'm not going anywhere."

Papa, I thought, would be so proud of me.

Jehu's shoulders seemed to relax. Was that a hint of admiration in his eyes?

Sootie smiled up at me. "Oh good! Now I can show you how to make me a dolly." She tugged at my hand.

Jehu snapped his fingers. "I almost forgot. I've got something for you," he said, fishing in the leather satchel slung over his shoulder and pulling out a letter. The handwriting was familiar.

"It's a letter—" he began.

"From Papa!" I cried, snatching it from his fingers.

"Picked it up from a passing ship. Got a few letters for Swan, and one for Russell, too."

The mail was a random enterprise, with letters generally delivered by passing ships. I had not received a letter from Papa since arriving on Shoalwater Bay. Then again, I had not written Papa for several months now, and as I turned the letter over in my hand, I felt a rush of guilt.

Although he had not prevented my trip, Papa had made it clear that he did not think highly of William Baldt, and I had delayed writing him from shame when William had not met me upon my arrival. I had intended to write him after William showed up and we were married. Then the engagement had been broken, and as I had thought to return home, there was no need for a letter. Now perhaps I would write and persuade Papa to join me. The settlement could most certainly use a proper physician.

Papa. How I missed his booming laugh. His warm eyes. His ability to finish off one of Mrs. Parker's cherry pies in a single sitting.

I recalled the way his mustache turned up at the corners when he smiled, and how he never turned away patients, not even when they stumbled onto our doorstep in the middle of the night.

And most of all, I recalled how when I was a little girl he would stand at the bottom of the stairs and call: "Where is my favorite daughter?"

It was our little ritual. I would throw back the covers on my four-poster bed, rush down the hall in my bare feet, and peer down at him from the top of the stairs.

"She is right here!" I would say. "And she is your *only* daughter!"

He would shake his head at me, his eyes crinkling with amusement, and more often than not, he would roar with laughter at the picture I presented.

"You're not my Janey! My Janey never sleeps through breakfast! My Janey's hair is never tangled."

It had always just been Papa and me. And, of course, Mrs. Parker, our kindly housekeeper, who had wiped away every childhood tear with her worn apron. They were all the family I had ever known.

I took the letter and carefully, slowly unfolded it, intending to savor every word.

February 15, 1854

My sweet Janey,

You cannot know how it pains me to write this letter.

How I would wish, rather, for one last chance to tell you that you are my favorite daughter.

I have been suffering from consumption these past months. Although it broke my heart to let you go, I knew that you would be safer away. I'm quite afraid that I could not bear the thought of you succumbing to this wretched illness as well. As such, I have left instructions for my solicitor, Mr. Edmonds, to send you this letter upon my death.

It has been a great comfort to me to know that you have begun a new life with William, and I wish you every happiness, my dearest girl. It was selfish of me to stand in your way those last months you were at home.

Please forgive an old man who could not bear to watch his little girl grow up and leave his house to start a home of her own. Your happiness is all I have ever longed for since you came into my life as a red-haired, smiling infant with a penchant for sucking on my thumb. Your bright face was the only thing that made life possible for me after your mother's death.

In regard to my estate, I have directed that Mr.
Edmonds sell the house on Walnut Street and give a portion
of the funds to Mrs. Parker, who may continue on as
housekeeper for the new owner if she so wishes. The rest of
the money shall be deposited in your account at the bank in
San Francisco. I fear that I have not left you a fortune, my
dear, but perhaps it will be enough to buy you some small
thing that your heart desires.

I have always loved you, Janey—both the little girl
who ran around with a pie-stained apron and tangled hair,
and the elegant young lady you have become.

Take greatest care of yourself, my dearest daughter.
Listen to your heart, and you will find your way.

Remember—you make your own luck.

Love, Papa

When I looked up, Jehu was standing there, watching me
carefully.

"Bad news?"

I shook my head wordlessly. Above us a gull squawked
hoarsely, and as if it were yesterday I recalled the way Papa's
coughing had filled the house at night, and how he had at first
forbidden me to travel west to marry William. What horrible
fights we had had! And then I recalled how, the morning after a
visit by a fellow physician, Papa's resistance had abruptly evapo-
rated, and he had given me his permission to marry.

He had known he was dying! That was why he had let me go.

I felt a pain deep in my stomach, sharp as the hurtful words I had spoken to my sweet papa, and staggered forward.

"Boston Jane?" Sootie asked nervously, looking between Jehu and me.

Jehu's eyes widened in alarm. "Jane, what is it?" he asked urgently, grabbing my shoulders.

"Papa's dead."

"Oh Jane." Jehu's voice echoed in my head.

And then I did precisely what Miss Hepplewhite would have recommended in just such a situation. I fainted.